Atlantic City Kaiju

and other short stories

Jonathan Altvater

You'd have to be a real asshole to quote yourself
at the beginning of your own book.
Jonathan Altvater

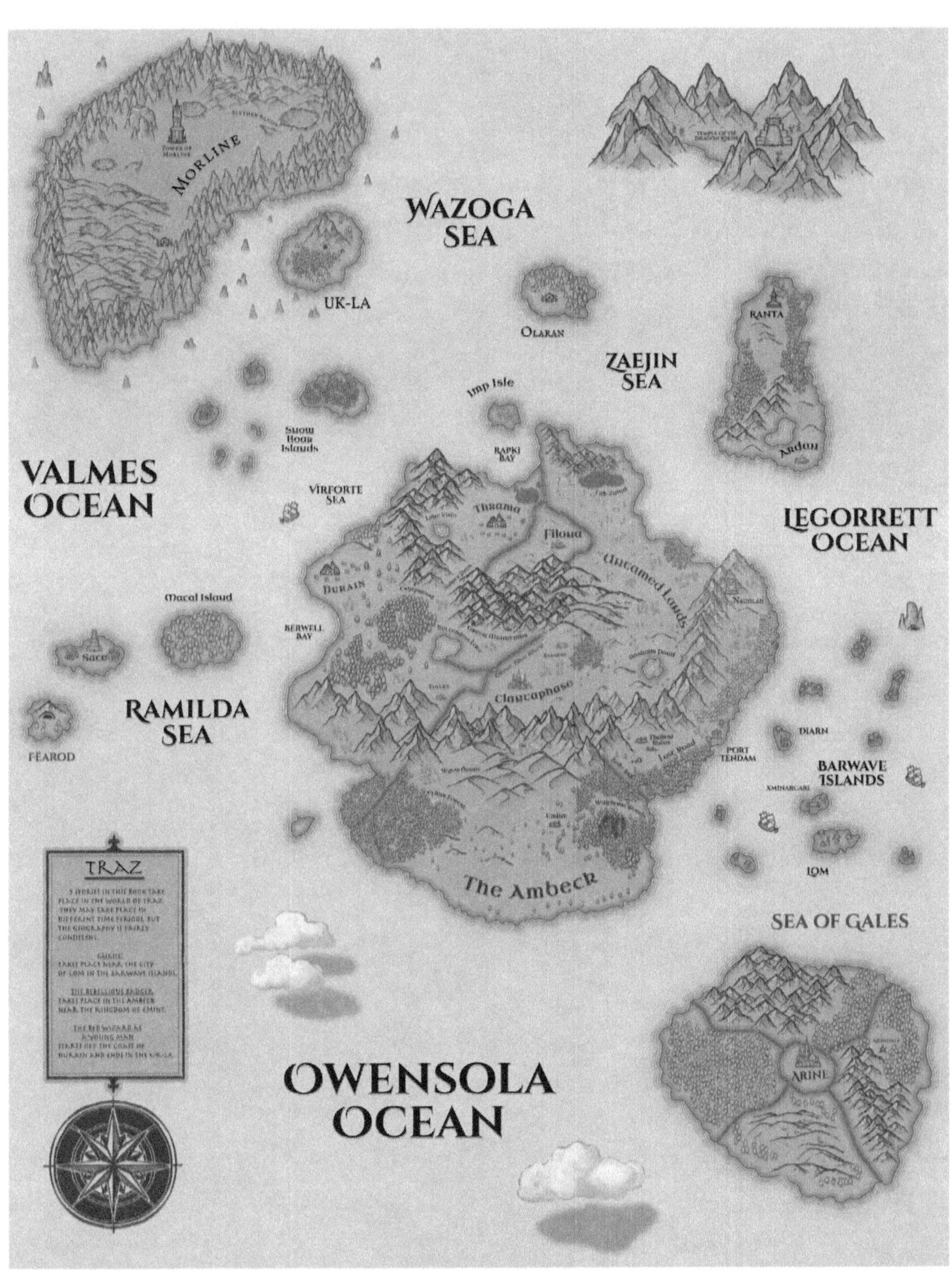

MORLINE
TOWER OF MORLINE
WAZOGA SEA
UK-LA
OLARAN
RANTA
ZAEJIN SEA
ARDON
IMP ISLE
RAPKI BAY
VALMES OCEAN
VIRFORTE SEA
THRAMA
FILOUA
UNTAMED LANDS
LEGORRETT OCEAN
DURAIN
NAIMLAN
MACAL ISLAND
BERWELL BAY
SACO
RAMILDA SEA
CLANTAPHASE
DIARN
BARWAVE ISLANDS
FEAROD
PORT TENDAM
XMINARGARL
LOM
THE AMBECK
SEA OF GALES
TRAZ
ARINE
OWENSOLA OCEAN

A GOOD START

Ryan Abernathy sat on the toilet, naked except for an old coffee-stained Beastie Boys shirt. He looked to his right. There was half a roll of toilet paper. It was a good start.

"How long have I been here?" He asked himself.

Probably a few minutes. It felt like hours. It felt like the past hour had been split into miniature lifetimes. He had smoked too much weed. Every moment was a snapshot with a story that ended with him wondering how much time had passed.

Ryan looked to his right. There was half a roll of toilet paper. It was a good start.

"Oh, I'm still here," he thought. He sniffed. It smelled bad. "I must be done," he quietly said to himself. No one likes a party pooper, or someone who spends the party pooping, or poop in general. No one likes that. Well, maybe the scat crowd. Ryan made a disgusted face.

He looked to his right. There was half a roll of toilet paper. It was a good start.

The house party he was at was insane. When the place was popping there must have been a hundred people in that tiny apartment. Maybe even a hundred and three! There was this weird DJ kid who kept all his equipment in a red radio flyer wagon. The equipment was jerry rigged to a car battery. The DJ kid was tall and pale with a short scraggly beard. Among the crowd was an older Iraq war vet freestyling nonsense raps into a yellow Fisher-Price microphone. The microphone was connected to a guitar amp with the distortion cranked. The rumor going around the party was that the DJ and the rapper were homeless. How rad is that?

He looked to his right. There was half a roll of toilet paper. It was a good start. Ryan reached out to the toilet paper roll and started spinning it.

After the party, people left and there were only about eight or nine late-night party goers. This was when the chill shit started. It was all beers, weed, and philosophy. Ryan partook in all three. He was a philosophy major in college, after all.

Out on the back porch the discussion was heating up. Batman versus Spider-Man. Who wins in a fight? Does Batman have prep time? Is it in Queens or Gotham City? Why are they fighting? Oh man, it could go on forever!

There was a cute skater girl named Sherry Bomb sitting to Ryan's right. It was a good start. She seemed to agree with him about the Batman advantage. Sherry was really pretty. As everyone continued arguing, she slowly crept closer to him. She lightly kicked Ryan's shoe in a flirtatious kind of way. He'd look at her and Sherry would smile and laugh and look down. It was adorable.

He looked to his right. There was half a roll of toilet paper. It was a good start.

"Damn," Ryan muttered to himself. Something stirred in the bathtub. He wrapped the toilet paper around his hand and wiped his ass. All clean! He wondered how long he had been in there. He wondered if Sherry was still there.

When he was outside on the porch, two of the other philosophers were reenacting the epic fight between Bats and Spidey. Of course, being a biased third party, Ryan had to evaluate the epic crossover struggle. He was happily just watching, and rolled his eyes when he was pulled up to be the referee. He wanted to spend more time with the girl. Maybe he'd get some for once. It had been a long dry spell. The battle must have raged on for decades. He questioned how long he watched those two tumble in the grass homoeroticly at least three times.

He looked to his right. There was half a roll of toilet paper. He wasn't sure what the significance was. I mean, he already wiped his ass, but there it was.

A small snore came from the bathtub. Ryan stood up. Where the fuck were his pants?

"Damn," he muttered again.

After Batman won (the battle, not the war), Ryan went looking for Sherry. He had this great Tony Hawk joke that he wanted to tell her. Then he was going to grind her like Tony Hawk would have. That was the joke. In retrospect, it wasn't that great a joke, but they were both drunk and high so maybe it would have scored him hunk points. We'll never know because he found her kissing that homeless DJ kid in the kitchen!

"Oh nooooooo…," Ryan said into the mirror as he washed his face in the bathroom with his dick and balls dangling by his thighs.

He looked to his left. There was half a roll of toilet paper. He was glad it still existed. Someday, someone might need to poop again....

He wondered how long he had been in that bathroom - probably a thousand years. All the humans had most likely died off. The earth had crumbled and there was just this bathroom floating in the void of space with Ryan, whoever was in the bath- tub, and that half roll of toilet paper.

The toilet paper would have to last. It was the last roll in the universe. Ryan began to smile. He had already gone a millen- nium and still had plenty left. Enough for at least five thousand years. That is, unless the tub guy woke up and needed to shit. Then it might not last as long.

Wait a minute. Who's in the tub? Ryan was curious. They had drifted so far through space together. How long had it been? Probably, ten minutes. He smoked way too much weed. Time was acting weird.

When he pulled back the curtain he saw that it was the DJ sleeping in the tub. His shirt was gone, his pants were around his ankles and there was a used condom in the soap dish.

Thus, began the deductions of Detective Ryan Abernathy. Let's look for clues!

- Mostly naked dude in the tub
- Seen earlier with one Miss Sherry Bomb making out in the kitchen.
- Used condom
- Half used roll of toilet paper

It was a good start.

Now one could conclude that Miss Sherry Bomb and the DJ kid scrumped in the bathtub. One could deduce that DJ kid went to take a shower, forgot to take off his pants, tripped over them, fell perfectly into the tub as he hit his head and knocked himself out. But what of the condom? Jizz gnomes? Nah. They probably did it in the tub. It must have been uncomfortable. It was a small tub. Maybe they did it standing up?

"Damn," Ryan muttered to himself.

How long had he been standing there looking at this naked dude in the tub? Two, maybe three thousand years? Is that gay? Ryan looked down at his weiner. Still soft! That's ok then. It's procedural. Like a doctor examining a naked dude. Where the fuck were Ryan's pants? Where was the homeboy's shirt? Was there some guy out there wearing both of their clothes? Assuming their identities? Like a shitty fusion clone! My god, why was Ryan still looking at his weiner? I guess we'll find out NEXT TIME ON DRAGON BALL Z!

He had to solve the case! Yeah, he banged her in the bathtub. They were probably standing up.

Case closed!

So now what? What was so great about this guy? He's homeless. Ryan lived down the block in a rented house. Point Ryan. Ryan still had a shirt. Point Ryan. Homeboy still technically had his pants even though he wasn't wearing them. Point DJ kid. He also banged Sherry in the shower. A thousand points DJ kid. Damn, DJ kid won. 1001 Points To Ryan's 2.

What if....

What if Ryan peed on him? It would probably be satisfying. I mean his dick was already out. Serves him right for stealing his girl. Nah, she wasn't his girl. He was drunk and high and acting like a loser. Best to cut his losses. Ryan sighed and reached down to zip up his pants. He wasn't wearing any.

"Just go to bed Ryan," he said to himself as he opened the bathroom door and briefly looked at the half roll of toilet paper. Still there. It was a pretty lame ending to the night, but it had a good start.

THE END

CLICHÉ

She was blond and tan. Normally she would be fair-skinned, but she had spent the last few years outside. Today would be no different.

The sun felt hot as it beamed itself onto her shapely body. She dug her toes deep into the damp sand. It was cool and refreshing. Now and then a wave would wash up and tickle her ankles. It felt good to be on land again, but she could never be far from the sea. She shared a connection with it. It gave her freedom.

She had spent the day exploring the little town by the beach. The girl mapped it all out in her head. The locations of the pawnshops, mansions, banks, and bars were all tucked away in her meticulous brain. She also saw that the town's defenses were lax at best. Picking this village's riches clean would be no harder than picking grapes off their stems.

That would be tomorrow. Today the crew was on shore leave. Today it was all about drinking beer on the beach and soaking up rays. She let out a content sigh as she looked out over the endless sea. Then she saw the white sails.

"Who the fuck is that?" she said to herself. She stood up, took off her sunglasses, and strained her eyes to get a better look at the emblem on the sail. She frowned. "Black Knife pirates? Here? Now? Really?" she mumbled. The girl shook her head in disgust as she put her sunglasses on and sat back down on her beach chair. She lit a cigar. "What a bunch of fucking posers," she thought. The girl reached into her ice bucket and pulled out another beer. After unscrewing it, placed the tip on her lips, and within seconds, had downed half the bottle. The cigar never left her lips. She closed her eyes as that fuzzy drunk feeling took hold.

It was a good buzz. She belched.

When she opened her eyes the landing boats were rowing to shore. Each pirate had a bandana tied around their heads - every single one of them wore an eye patch. One of them wore two eye patches. A wave hit and he almost fell out of the boat. Half of them had hooks for hands. The other half had parrots on their shoulders.

"You gotta be kidding me," she said to herself with a smirk. Two of the boats accidentally crashed into one another.

"Yar! Watch where ye be goin ya flea bitten scallywag!" one of the pirates growled.

"Go fuck ye self and your mudder da whore!" another pirate responded in kind. The first pirate stood up and swung his oar at the man in the other boat. He didn't even come close to hitting him, but he did manage to lose his balance and fall overboard. Everybody laughed. The girl on the beach put her hand to her forehead and chuckled to herself.

"I can't believe I'm about to lose all my gold to these idiots," she moaned.

Finally, after three more boat crashes and two more water-logged pirates, they came ashore. Most of them ran right past the girl on the beach and began ransacking the town. The poor town - it never stood a chance, even against these clumsy pirates. The girl just sighed and finished her beer. She laid back in her little striped beach chair and closed her eyes. She let the warmth of the sun and the buzz of her beer wash over her.

"Yar!!" said a voice. It was loud and shrill.

The girl opened her eyes and saw a pirate in a white puffy shirt. He had a polka dot bandana on his head. He also had an eye patch over his right eye of course. The sun gleamed off of the hook coming out of his right shirt sleeve. His other hand pointed a sword at her jugular. The girl rolled her eyes at him, but he didn't notice because of her dark sunglasses. She smiled at him mischievously.

"Can you please get out of my sun," she complained. "I'm trying to enjoy my day off." He looked perplexed.

"Ain't ye be seeing what's going on around ya wench? The Black Knife Pirates be me mates proper and we be sacking your petty little village!" he growled.

"Well, yo ho ho then! Good luck with that," she said. Her voice was dripping with sarcasm.

"Such sass! Pretty though! I should bound yer hands and take ye aboard the ship as me trophy. All the boys could have a go at ya! How does that sound ya bilge brat?" he growled angrily.

"Sounds kind of hot honestly," she said. "Why don't we go into that alley behind us and you give me a quick scrump before we leave?"

"Really?" he managed to mutter. He was shocked. Had his pirate charm worked? Was this girl really so in heat that she'd let him poke her with his snickerdoodle?

"Yeah sure, let's go," she said as she put out her cigar in the sand. She opened another beer and chugged the bottle. After she belched, she slung her backpack around her shoulder then grabbed his hook gently and led him into the alley just inside the town's walls.

The two buildings making the alley were made out of orange adobe clay. It was midafternoon and the sun was on its way down. It made yellow triangles appear on the walls in contrast to the cool shade. The ground was still sandy and little beach weeds stuck out at their feet.

She pressed her body to his and pushed him against the wall. She removed her sunglasses, revealing her aquamarine eyes. They were the color of the sea in the shallows. She gave him a mischievous smile. Her mouth was so close to his that he could smell the beer on her breath. She closed her eyes and he did the same.

"Promise me one thing, big boy," she whispered.

"Anything," he said.

"Try not to get any blood on my new bikini," she continued.

"Is this your first time?" he asked.

"No, I do this all the time," she said happily as she head-butted him. She broke his nose. She jumped back just in time to avoid the waterfall of blood dripping down all over his white puffy shirt.

Then she started punching him. She mostly hit him in the face, but it wouldn't be fair if we failed to mention his cracked ribs. There *were* some body shots too. She focused her attention on his eye patch. Her bare hands felt like hammers as they crashed into his skull. She suspected that he wore that eye patch for show, but there was no doubt that he would be wearing that eyepatch for the rest of his life. If there was an eye, she destroyed it.

She stopped punching him when it felt like she was hitting raw meat. His body collapsed to the ground face first. The girl looked down at her bloody hands. She examined her white bikini. There were some blood splatters on her arms and her belly, but surprisingly, there was no blood on her suit.

"Maybe you aren't so bad after all, buddy," she said to the unconscious man. "Guess this means I'm not going to kill you." She examined him. He landed on his face and there was no blood on the back of his shirt. She took this opportunity to wipe the blood off her hands. The back of his bandana was torn open, and he had a little bit of red on it. That probably happened when she head-butted him. He had his back against the wall after all. She also noticed that the hook was fake. His hand was in his sleeve, holding a handle with a hook on the end the whole time. She sat against the wall and lit another cigar. The girl closed her eyes and enjoyed the shade for a little while.

The man started to wake up. He coughed up blood and spat it on the ground in front of him. He hurt all over. His face was beginning to swell and throbbed numbly.

"Good afternoon, sport. Did you enjoy your nap?" she teased as he struggled to sit up. He leaned his back against the wall and turned to her.

"I guess this means we're not having sex?" he smiled as he turned to her.

"Nah kid, you never stood a chance," she replied. She stood up and turned around to grab her backpack. The bloody pirate checked out her butt. She had a nice bubble booty. Then he noticed the tattoo. This woman had a tattoo of a bloody dragon wing on her right shoulder blade.

"That tattoo. You're..." he started to say.

"That's right. I'm the one they call Blood Wing," she replied. "I'm the captain of The Joyous Plunder. Tell the captain of the Black Knives that I'm coming after him."

To Hell and Back

Blood Wing made it back to The Joyous Plunder when the sun was low in the sky. It was a medium-sized pirate ship with two black sails. They proudly displayed the crew's jolly roger. It was a smiling skull wearing a crown. Below the skull, there was a bright red bow tie. Despite it's comical nature, it struck fear into all that saw the jolly roger cresting with the waves on the high sea. An ornate railing ran along the side of the Joyous Plunder's deck. Cannons stuck out their black hollow noses on the sides, and on the bow of the boat, large iron spikes protruded forward.

The pirate queen walked out into the surf and began to swim back to her ship. The water felt cool and refreshing after a long day of baking in the sun. It was a shame they had to go to work tonight. The day had been so pleasant until the Black Knives reared their buffoonery late in the afternoon.

Aboard the ship a man and an elf were playing cards. Rather, the elf was teaching the man how to play. The elf was named Leaf. He was not of the high race, but his father was a great hero during Sword War II. His hair was moss green like most tree elves. He wore an old tan shirt that could have been made out of an old potato sack. If it wasn't for the ornate boomerang he wore at his side, Leaf could easily be mistaken for an elven hobo.

Unlike Leaf, the man sitting in front of him was well dressed. He wore a three-piece cream-colored business suit complete with a matching tie and black suspenders hidden under his jacket. On his head, he wore a grey beanie, and sported a thick blond beard. His name was Willy.

"See, what you would do here is turn your spell card sideways. That brings my life down three points," instructed Leaf as he adjusted the number on a twenty-sided die he had in front of him.

"Sounds complicated," Willy said. "Do we have to play this tonight? Blackjack is so much easier."

"Cap said we could play elf games tonight. Gerald learned quickly when I taught him and so did Stacks and Jean. You are the only one protesting," replied Leaf. He seemed a little annoyed.

"Stacks don't ever talk! How would he even be capable of protesting?" exasperated Willy.

Stacks was within earshot of the exchange. He was a large, muscular man. Stacks stomped his foot loudly to get their attention and then gave Willy the finger before walking down to a lower deck.

"He seems pretty good at protesting to me," said Leaf. "Now draw a card." Willy rolled his eyes and grabbed a card. He looked out and saw Blood Wing swimming up to the boat.

"Cap's back," he announced.

"Good, that means we can get this game going and I can win back all that money I lost to you last week when we played poker," said Leaf.

"I tried to teach you how to play, but you just weren't having it," said Willy.

"Sounds familiar," said Leaf.

The captain climbed onto the deck and a man handed her a towel. It was Gerald. Gerald was by far the most capable of the crew aside from Blood Wing. He was the first one to join and also happened to be the first mate.

"Thanks Gerald," she said as she dried the salty water from her hair. "I'm going to go get dressed. Round up the boys. We need to have a talk."

"Are we in trouble?" he asked.

"No, but we're about to go find some," she said as she handed him back the towel.

•••

The crew all gathered by the mast of the ship in front of the high deck. Blood Wing came out of her cabin dressed for war - wearing a black bandana and her hair tied into two long braids that went down to her hips. On each arm, she wore leather bracers with an iron mesh sewn into it. A leather belt hung casually from her hips over her green camouflage pants. The belt holstered two large knives and a one shot flintlock handgun. The crew was surprised to see her dressed up like this. Tonight was supposed to be a casual night of drinking and gambling.

"What is she up to?" Gerald said with a smirk.

The captain grinned at her curious crew and turned around. She climbed the steps to the higher deck, thinking about what she was about to say. When she reached the top, she turned back to them and leaned forward on the wooden railing in front of her.

"How are you guys doing?" she asked.

"Um, we're doing ok cap. How are you?" answered Willy.

"Oh, I'm alright, I suppose. Could be better. Nice weather we're having, eh?" she asked.

"Yes, there has been a nice cool breeze all day," said an old man in the back. The sun was setting behind her. The sky seemed to be on fire with bright yellows and pinks and reds. She became a silhouette in front of it.

"So, I was in town today," she began. "The place is easy pickings! So easy, that the Black Knife Pirates came ashore and looted it in broad daylight." There was a brief pause.

"Those fucks! They stole our mark!" yelled a pirate in the back with a badass facial scar.

"No, Jean, they became our mark," corrected Blood Wing. "The way I see it, there's a ship full of gold sailing east tonight. It's probably sailing pretty slow because it's weighed down with all that cargo. The pirates on board are amateurs at best."

"Aw cap, but we were going to play cards tonight," whined

Leaf.

"Come on, Leaf! Imagine how much gold you'll have after you win Willy's share tomorrow night! There's no way he will beat you at that elf card game!" she teased. Leaf nodded in approval. Willy rolled his eyes. Everyone else had a good laugh.

"Ok, everyone, we're going to war tonight! The one who brings in the most skrilla gets to spend the night with me in the captain's quarters!" she said while making her most seductive pose.

They all cheered! In their heads, they all knew that their captain had some strange loophole in place that would prevent them from ever sleeping in her cabin, but a glimmer of hope is a surprisingly strong motivation. That said, they would follow her to hell and back regardless.

Gold, Greed, and Glory

Willy sat in the crow's nest above the sails and stared out into the dark sea. What a strange turn his life had taken in the last four months. One minute he was brawling in the streets of Clantaphase for money, the next he was riding the tides with Blood Wing and her crew. The pay was great and he got beat up less. Overall, he didn't regret it. It just wasn't something he considered until it was presented to him. Life is like that sometimes. Out in the distance he saw a small orange glow.

"There they are," he muttered to himself. He opened the little hatch on the floor of the crow's nest and began his descent down the mast to the deck. Jean met him at the bottom.

"You got something?" Jean asked.

"Yeah, go tell the cap that their ship is at 10 o'clock. I'm going back up to scout some more," Willy responded as he began climbing back up.

Gerald was on the high deck steering the ship while Blood Wing chit chatted with him and drank coffee.

"So what do we know about these Black Knife Pirates?"

asked Gerald.

"I hear their captain is pretty strong, but I witnessed his crew and I doubt you guys will have any trouble beating them," she said.

"So, you're taking on their captain?" Asked Gerald.

"It wouldn't be any fun for me if I didn't," said Blood Wing. Gerald smirked.

"That's my cap!" He said. Jean walked up.

"Willy said the ship is at 10 o'clock," he said.

"Thanks Jean, I'm on it," replied Gerald. Jean nodded and went back to the lower deck to prep the cannons.

"Willy seems to be working out ok huh?" asked Blood Wing.

"Yeah, he seems like a good dude. No complaints here," said Gerald. "So, what's the plan tonight?"

"It's pretty obvious from what I said. A straight-up smash and grab. No prisoners. A lot of gold," answered the captain. Gerald smiled.

"The smashing part has me worried," he admitted.

"Oh, yes. We are going to ram their ship," she said with a mischievous smile. "I mean, we just installed those iron spikes on the bow."

"Nadine is going to hate this," said Gerald.

"She'll get over it," Blood Wing said with a wink.

•••

Captain Krunch was all smiles. This was the score he had dreamt of his entire life. He sat among piles of gold and jewels from plundering that afternoon. A large ruby caught his eye. It was hard to believe that all this was his. Krunch grabbed the ruby and squeezed it tightly in his palm before polishing it with his blue jacket. He held it up to the candlelight and admired how clear and perfect it was. Then he licked it. It tasted like a rock.

All this had to come at a price. Krunch knew it. He was a firm believer in karma. When one of his guys came back bloody and broken saying that Blood Wing was coming for him, Krunch laughed it off, but deep down inside he was frightened. He couldn't shake that feeling of dread. Of course the universe wanted him to pay his dues. He heard someone stomping down the stairs at the cargo hold.

"Ay captain, there be something outside ya may wanna be seeing!" growled a man with an eyepatch and a parrot.

"Here it comes," Krunch thought.

"My name is Bonita, and I want some tequila," squawked the parrot.

The two men and the parrot made their way out of the cargo hold and onto the deck. It was a calm and clear night. The air was cool, and the stars were exceptionally twinkly. The pirate with the parrot handed Krunch a telescope. "Look over yonder," he growled.

Krunch didn't need a telescope. It was easy to see that there was a ship approaching. He wondered why it took them so long to notice it. Blood Wing's ship would crash into them in a matter of minutes.

"Hey, big boy, want a hand job?" squawked the parrot.

"Alright. Launch a volley from the cannons!" commanded Krunch.

"Aye aye Captain! These scurvy dogs won't know what hit em!" growled the cliché.

"Back door costs extra!!!" yelled the parrot.

•••

"Hey Cap, they're firing their cannons at us," Gerald calmly said.

"Where the hell are they aiming? Do they even know how cannons work?" laughed Blood Wing. "Just keep heading straight at them."

"Nadine is gonna hate this. Why don't we just shoot them with our cannons? We know how to aim them," Gerald replied.

"Why waste gunpowder?" said Blood Wing. "Trust me, it'll

be fine." She winked at him and started making her way up to the bow of the boat.

"Cap, where are you…" Gerald started to say, but Blood Wing just waved him off without looking back. She was her own woman. Changing her mind was sometimes harder than turning the tide. Best to go with the flow.

She stood at the helm of the ship just above the spikes and drew the gun from her belt. It was a one-shot flintlock pistol. The weapon was a great surprise in a knife fight, but Blood Wing loathed reloading. It disrupted her battle flow. With one eye closed, she aimed at a cliché poser pirate on the next ship. He had a hook for a right hand, and he used it to carefully scratch his butt. She smirked. Killing him was kind of doing him a favor. One of these days, this fake pirate would probably get that hook stuck in his asshole. That would be so embarrassing. Best to kill him now so he could die with some dignity. She squeezed the trigger, and his head exploded just before the ships crashed.

Now she was flying. The impact launched her forward. In one swift motion, she holstered her gun and pulled out two large red knives. Each crimson blade was two feet long from hilt to blade. When she landed she pivoted with her ankle and went into a fast dash. Her knives became red blurs as she reached a fake pirate with a trimmed brown beard. She left him as fast as she arrived. He fell to his knees desperately trying to hold his guts inside his body.

One by one the Black Knife Pirates learned what made a ruthless pirate so feared. It wasn't growling and speaking the common tongue poorly. It wasn't hooks, or eye patches, or peg legs, or parrots that were obviously stolen from brothels. It was gold, greed, and glory. It's about not letting anything stand in your way to get what you want. It's not about talking a big game. It's about having a big game. It's a shame most of them never got the opportunity to apply this lesson to their lives.

The rest of Blood Wing's crew boarded the crippled ship. If Blood Wing had been the only one to board, the result would be a devastating defeat to The Black Knife Pirates. Now with the rest of her crew fighting, a full on massacre ensued. The Black Knife Pirates had no skill whatsoever.

•••

Krunch watched as his crew was slaughtered one by one. He wasn't particularly attached to any of them. They were all pathetic fanboys that he picked up in random bars. His plan was simple:

1. Build a crew
2. Plunder a town
3. Fuck over his crew
4. Keep all the gold for himself

He didn't need to bother about No3. His crew was dead, but now he would have to beat Blood Wing in a fight. Gods be damned. Was he strong enough to defeat The Virgin Queen of the Sea? He honestly didn't want to find out, but it seemed that fate had dealt him a hand that forced him to do so. He balled up his fist and began to run.

•••

Leaf held his steel boomerang above his head, and it began to glow a white green light. Down came his arm and the release sent the blade flying. It flew through the air, darting and swirling chaotically. Leaf was controlling it with his mind. It decapitated a man. It slashed open another man's belly. The men began to scatter.

Blood Wing was moving from pirate to pirate slicing their guts open as she flew by. Hot red liquid poured onto the ship's bow, and the wooden planks soaked it in.

"So, you are the infamous Blood Wing. I must admit, I'm not disappointed," said Captain Krunch as he approached her.

"Who the hell are you supposed to be?" Asked Blood Wing as she looked him up and down. She marveled at his ridiculously large hat.

"Pleased ta make ye acquaintance. I be Thadeus Krunch," he said.

"Who?" She asked.

"The captain of this here ship!" He yelled.

"I guess that explains the dumb hat," she laughed.

"My hat isn't dumb! My hat be awesome! You be the dumb one lass!" He yelled back.

"Nice comeback. I'm really impressed," she said with a wink.

"Shut up bitch!" He said.

"I'm so sorry. I didn't mean to hurt your fragile feelings. Look, your crew is pretty much dead at this point. My guys should have this wrapped up soon. Are you going to give up the gold, or are we going to do the thing where we fight, and I kill ya?" She asked. Blood Wing's crew began to gather around.

"We are going to fight," said Krunch. He was so fucked. He knew he couldn't pull this off. Even if he did pull this off somehow, there was no way he could take on the rest of her crew. Not unless he used *that technique* to win.

"Alright, I guess..." Blood Wing started.

"Fisticuffs," Krunch interrupted.

"A good old fashioned fistfight. Okay," she said as she sheathed her blades. Blood Wing pulled an old rag out of her pocket and used it to wipe the dead pirate blood off her face. This was his chance! Her guard was down. He lunged at her, but she spun behind him. "Eager to start, eh?"

Blood Wing was fast, but her spin had her off balance. She took a swing at him, and she had to put all her weight into it for her punch to connect. Unfortunately, it also made her punch exaggerated and easy to read. Krunch dodged just in time.

Now let's be honest here. Krunch was outmatched, but he was also an above-average fighter. The fact that Blood Wing was underestimating him worked in his favor. With Blood Wing again off-balance from her missed punch, he had just enough time to counter with a quick jab to her stomach. Then he used *that technique.*

What was *that technique* you ask? Well, it isn't anything too crazy. You see, when Krunch was a teenager, he had spent a year in Ranta being a bandit. He partnered up with a fighter named Celgado who happened to be an elf from Arine. The elves of Arine lived far from the tower in the capital at a forest monastery. They birthed a fighting style where they channeled their life magic into the blades of brandished weapons. Celgado developed a fighting style where he channeled that same energy into his fist. While Krunch was in the bandit game, he learned *that technique* from him. The problem was, Krunch wasn't an elf. So, when Krunch used it, his life was shortened. Elves are immortal creatures, so using life force didn't do them any harm.

Krunch used *that technique* against Blood Wing. The punch connected. She took it on the jaw, and it knocked her right on her ass.

"Oh shiiiiit!" Yelled Leaf.

"He hit the cap! That never happens!" Said Gerard. She slowly got up and spat blood on the deck.

"Lucky hit," she said. Then she ran at him, did a handstand, and kicked him with both legs right in the face. He flew up, then down, and landed on the deck. He was out cold.

***

Krunch awoke with his hands bound behind his back. It took him a minute to focus. He probably had a concussion. There was an orange light a little off in the distance. He squinted and blinked until it came into focus. He was looking at his ship in flames and sinking into the sea.

"Pretty, ain't it?" Said a voice from behind him. It was Blood Wing. She was smoking a cigar and cutting up an apple at a little table on her ship's deck.

"That ship was all I had. There it goes, bubbling into the deep," he sighed.

"For what it's worth, you pack a pretty good punch. It's not often that someone gets a hit off on me. It's too bad your crew had the fighting capability of a drunken toddler," she said.

"Cut the crap. What are you gonna do to me?" Krunch asked.

"Hey, guys! He's awake!" She yelled. Blood Wing's crew started to gather around. "Alright Krunchy, seeing that you and your crew are the most cliché group of pirates I have ever seen, we will be disposing of you in the most cliché way possible. You, my friend," she paused for a second to bask in her cleverness. "You are going to walk the plank!" Her crew cheered.

"Do we even have a plank?" Asked Jean.

"You bet your ass we do! Krunch had one on his ship, because of course he did, and I stole it! Stacks! Get over here! Bring that bad boy out!" Blood Wing said. She was enjoying this. Stacks came out from the cabin with a large ornate wooden plank. It had wooden carvings of elvish runes artfully adorning the long piece of wood. Leaf walked up and started reading the elvish lettering.

"Wow, this is great," he said. "The runes read 'Fuck You! Walk into the Blue!'"

"They do?!" Laughed Blood Wing. "That's awesome! Nail it down Stacks. We got us a plank!" Stacks placed the ornate plank on the deck, so half of it was hanging off the boat's side. He began nailing it to the deck.

"Ya know, Cap," said Willy, "I've been running with you guys for a couple of months now, but I'm not sure I've ever felt like a pirate. Now though, since we got a plank, I feel like a pirate."

"Well you better feel like a pirate because you are a pirate. You are honestly an excellent pirate. This guy Krunch, not so much," said Blood Wing. With that, she grabbed Krunch by his belt and brought the captured captain to his feet.

"Oh, I think it's time this guy moseyed off this plank," teased Gerald. Stacks put in the final nail and gave everyone a thumbs up. Blood Wing pulled Krunch in front of the plank and kicked him in the ass. It took all of Krunch's concentration not to fall off. He was still dizzy from the concussion, but he stayed standing on the edge of a watery demise.

"Okay, Captain," said Blood Wing, "Do you have any last

words before you take a dip?"

"You haven't seen the last of me, Blood Wing!" He said as he jumped off the plank.

"Did he really just say that?!" Laughed Blood Wing. She had both hands on the sides of her head marveling at how cliché that was.

"He just said that," confirmed Gerald.

"Wow. Okay. He's gonna come up for air soon and when he does, we're gonna pull out our guns and we're going to shoot him," said Blood Wing. She smiled and winked at the crew. They nodded and pulled out their pistols. Seconds later, Krunch's body was riddled with holes. The water around him turned red. That was the last they ever saw of him.

***

Later that night, the crew of The Joyous Plunder drank ale, partied late, and played card games to celebrate their victory. Leaf won most of Willy's gold in the card game. Everyone else pretty much broke even. They sang pirate songs like Barwave Wench, Beat Em Up, and Baby Got Back. At one point a drunken Blood Wing got up and made a speech.

"You guys are the best," she started. "That's why I picked ya to join me on this blood-stained little adventure we're on. We're going to be rich when this is all over. Because if the going gets tough, we kill those mother fuckers. Anyway, good job tonight."

"Who brought back the most gold?" Willy yelled from the back.

"Oh yeah, the sexy contest!" She said. "I brought back the most gold. So, I guess I'm sleeping alone in the captain's cabin tonight." The crew rolled their eyes, but they knew no one would get to bunk up with her. They knew that before they set sail today.

Blood Wing retired to her cabin soon after. She nestled up in bed with her arms around a bag of gold.

"Aren't you handsome?" She said as she began to seduce

the bag of coins. She stripped naked and began to rub the coins all over her body. After a brief moment of ecstasy, she began to quiver and fell asleep drunk, satisfied, and happy to be alive. It was a long and dreamless sleep.

The End

THE REBELLIOUS BADGER

A Folktale of The Ambeck

Long ago in The Ambeck there was a great castle and in it lived a great king. He had many subjects and all the riches and luxuries that he desired. Under his rule, the kingdom grew and thrived. No one questioned his rule because everyone was very well fed and the ale flowed freely.

When the king died, he left his prosperous state to his son. The people mourned their king, but felt they were in good hands because their new king was his father's son. Surely he would follow his father's exemplary rule, and rule justly too.

The new king was not as clever as his father. His subjects went on with their lives, but after some seasons passed, they began to notice that there was less food in their coffers and the ale did not flow as freely as it once had. Some began to speak against their king, but only in the forests and fields away from the king's ears.

One day the miller and the shoemaker were walking through the forest. They stopped at an old tree and decided to sit down and eat a pie. As they ate, they joked about the king's incompetence.

A badger lived in a hole at the base of the tree and smelled the delicious pie. He decided to come out and greet the miller and the shoemaker. The two men did not notice the badger at first, so they continued to mock their king.

"I say, the king is dumb as shit," said the shoemaker. "He does not know his mouth from his asshole, for he speaks from his ass and he eats with his ass as well!"

"How does one eat with his ass?" Asked the miller.

"One does so by sticking a carrot in their bottom," replied the shoe maker.

"If he eats and speaks from his ass, what does he use his mouth for?" Asked the miller.

"Sucking dicks!" The shoemaker laughed.

"Oh snap!" Said the miller. They both had a good giggle. The badger had a good laugh as well and was when the two men noticed him.

"Lo, mister badger. To what do we owe the pleasure?" Asked the shoemaker.

"I smelled your delicious pie. Since you are having a sit in front of my tree, I was hoping you could spare me a slice," said the badger.

"I would be happy to share this pie if you were to share some badger wine," said the shoemaker.

"Ah yes, I do have a nice bottle in my tree. Give me a moment and I shall fetch it for us," said the badger before he scurried back to his home. He came back out moments later with three goblets and a bottle of badger wine. The shoemaker cut the badger a slice of pie, and the three of them ate, drank, and were merry.

"Do the people of your kingdom ever tire of watching your king speak from his ass and stick carrots in his bottom? Do they tire of watching him suck dicks? You would think a king would spend his time ruling his kingdom instead of acting this way," said the badger.

"Are you kink-shaming our king, mister badger?" Asked the miller.

"That was not my intention. It is just a waste of good carrots and you are not the first people to walk through my forest who speak ill of him. One may suck dicks as they please, but talking shit is not a good quality for a king. Why is it that you do not rise up against him and remove him from his throne?" Asked the badger.

"There are too many who remain loyal to him. They have fond memories of his father," said the shoemaker.

"I am very clever," stated the badger. "If you follow my lead, I can win over the hearts and minds of your people. We could rise against him and instill a new king."

"Mister badger," laughed the miller. "You have shared your wine with us and for that I am grateful. I am enjoying your company, but you are a badger. I do not think the people will rally around you."

"If I was a man, I could overthrow the government in thirty-one days," said the badger

"Perhaps you could, but while you are a very clever badger, you are still a badger. Should you ever become a man, my axe would be in your service, but for now I am content to call you friend and eat and drink with you," said the shoemaker.

"Miller, would you pledge your sword to me if I were to become a man so we might overthrow the government?" Asked the badger.

"Ay, I would, but for now I am content to eat and drink with you as the one I call friend," said the miller.

The three of them ate and drank until they were out of pie and badger wine. The two men packed up and said their goodbyes to the badger. They stumbled home from the forest in a drunken haze.

A week later the red wizard Rune was walking through the same forest and sat next to the badgers tree. He pulled out a pipe and began puffing on the dankest weed. The badger smelled it and came out to greet the wizard.

"Lo, mister badger! To what do I owe the pleasure?" Asked the wizard.

"I smelled your dank weed. Since you are having a sit in front of my tree, I was hoping you would spare me a puff," said the badger.

"I would be happy to share this pipe if you were to share some badger wine," said the wizard.

"Ah yes, I do have a nice bottle in my tree. Give me a moment and I shall fetch it for us," said the badger before he scurried to his home. He came back out moments later with two goblets and a bottle of badger wine. The wizard passed the pipe and the two of them smoked, drank, and were merry.

"I am new to this place. This is my first time south of the mountains. Tell me about this kingdom," said the wizard while packing more dank weed into the pipe.

"This land is a wild place. There are great worms in the desert to the north and foul packs of wolves if you venture further from the castle," said the badger.

"Ay," said the wizard. "I have seen the great worms. They are very dangerous. The desert is wide and it keeps this place isolated from the rest of the world. Tell me about the king in the castle beyond these trees."

"The king's father was a good and respected man. The current king is a fool and many of his subjects laugh at him behind his back," said the badger.

"What kind of things do they say?" The wizard asked.

"They say he does not know his mouth from his asshole. For he speaks from his ass and he eats with his ass as well," said the badger.

"How does one eat with their ass?" Asked the wizard with a smile.

"He sticks carrots in his bottom," said the badger.

"What does he use his mouth for?" Asked the wizard.

"Sucking dicks," said the badger. The wizard had a good laugh.

"You are a clever and funny little badger," said the wizard. "Your wine tastes heavenly, and I am happy to share my dank weed and call you friend. Now, tell me about the wolves in the forest."

"Oh, the wolves are quite interesting," said the badger. "By day they are men living in a secluded village. By night they become wolves who hunt in packs and kill animals like me. Once a month, when the moon is full, they become something in between. They stand on their hind legs and kill men and animals alike."

"Mister badger," said the wizard. "This is very good information for a wizard to have. I would like to see these wolves."

"If you want to see them, keep travelling east," said the badger. "Though, if I were you, I would steer clear of them."

"I will see them all the same because I am also very clever. I have decided to grant you a wish," said the wizard. "As long as it is within my power, I shall grant you anything you desire."

"I wish I were a man for 31 days so that I could overthrow the government," said the badger.

"This I can do. I will place an enchantment such that those who look upon you will see a man instead of a badger. However, be warned, on the 31st day, the enchantment will break, and you will be seen as a badger once again," the wizard said with a solemn voice.

"Can I be a handsome man?" Asked the badger.

"Of course," said the wizard. He waved his hands through the air and looked upon the handsome man who was once a badger. "Go forth and create mischief and I will do the same in the east."

The two said their goodbyes and parted ways as friends. The wizard traveled east and the man who was once a badger made his way into town.

When the man that was once a badger entered the town, he went straight to the shoemaker's house and knocked on the door. His wife answered.

"Well aren't you a handsome man," she said. "How can I help you?"

"Tell your husband that he and I once shared a drink, he pledged an oath to help me overthrow the government," said the man who was once a badger.

"He did, did he?" Asked the shoemaker's wife. "This should be interesting. Hold on one moment and I will fetch him." The shoemaker came to the door.

"How can I help you sir?" He asked.

"Friend shoemaker, you may not recognize me, but I am the badger who lives in the tree outside of town. I have met a wizard, and he has granted me the appearance of a man. May I come in so we may discuss overthrowing the government," said the man who was once a badger.

The startled shoemaker said, "Yes, but keep your voice down," as he let him into the house.

They drank beer and ate tasty cakes. At the end of the night, the shoemaker liked his plan. He would join the revolution. The man who was once a badger said goodbye to the shoemaker and made his way to the miller's house. He knocked on the miller's door and the miller's baby mama answered.

"Well aren't you a handsome man," said the miller's baby momma. "How can I help you?"

"Tell your baby daddy that he and I once shared a drink nd he made an oath to help me overthrow the government," said the man who was once a badger.

"That dopey son of a bitch always gets into trouble when he drinks," said the miller's baby momma. "Let me go fetch him." The miller came to the door.

"How can I help you?" Asked the miller.

"Friend miller, you may not recognize me, but I am the badger who lives in the tree outside of town. I have met a wizard, and he has granted me the appearance of a man. May I come in so we may discuss overthrowing the government?" Asked the man who was once a badger.

The startled miller said, "Yes, but keep your voice down," as he let him into the house.

They drank beer and ate fresh bread. At the end of the night, the miller liked his plan. He would join the revolution.

The next day, the three men met at the local tavern. The man who was once a badger stood on a table and began to speak.

"Today is a momentous day!" He yelled. "The next round of drinks is on me!" The shoemaker gave the barkeep a small sack of coins and everyone cheered as they were served up free drinks. A little later, the man who was once a badger stood on the table again and began to speak.

"Today is a momentous day!" He yelled. "The next round of drinks is on me!" The miller gave the barkeep a small sack of coins and everyone cheered as they were served up free drinks. More time had passed. Then the man who was once a badger stood on the table a third time. Everyone began to cheer.

"Are you all good and knackered?" He asked. Everyone in the tavern cheered. "Good because I have something I want to say. I am sick and tired of living in a kingdom where the king doesn't know his mouth from his asshole! A man who speaks with his ass and eats with it as well! I am sick of a king who sticks carrots in his bottom! I ask you, are your pantries as full as they once were?"

"No!" Yelled the crowd

"Does the ale flow as freely as it did in days passed?" The man who was once a badger asked.

"No!" Yelled the crowd.

"Then we must band together and overthrow this king! For he is leading us down a path where things can only get worse! Grab your swords! Grab your axes! We march on the castle tonight!" Yelled the man who was once a badger. The drunken mob roared with applause. They ran back to their homes and came back with weapons and torches.

Then they marched on the castle in a drunken stupor. When they arrived at the front gate they were stopped by the guards.

"Why are you coming to the king's castle with weapons and torches?" Asked the leader of the guards.

"We come to overthrow the king!" Said the man who was once a badger.

"Well, that's no good," said the guard. "It is my job to prevent you from bringing harm to the king. If you push further, we will be forced to cut down your drunken mob."

"Well, I don't want to bring any harm to these fine drunk individuals. Ask the king if he would speak with me," commanded the badger.

"I will speak with the king," said the leader of the guard. "Please wait here." The guard left and the drunken mob was surprisingly patient. They waited for the guard to return. Eventually he did.

"The king has agreed to an audience with you. Only you may enter the castle. The rest of you must go home and get some rest," said the guard leader. The drunken mob cheered for they were tired and wanted to go to bed.

"I shall speak with the king," yelled the man who was once a badger. "I will convince him to take the carrots out of his bottom and step down as king. Then we shall choose a new leader!" The crowd cheered as the guard who was once a badger was escorted into the castle. Then they stumbled home and passed out on their beds.

The guards led the man who was once a badger down a long hall. Once inside, he was tackled by the guards and was put in chains. They brought him down to the dungeon and threw him into a cell. He never did meet with the king. He rotted in his cage for 30 days.

On the afternoon of the 31st day, the red wizard Rune appeared in the man who would soon be a badger again's cell.

"How did your revolution go?" The wizard asked with a frown. "Did you overthrow the king who put carrots in his bottom and dicks on his mouth?"

"No. I asked to have an audience with him, and they brought me into the castle and threw me in this dungeon," said the man who had been a badger 31 days ago.

"Well, it serves you right! A kingdom must not be overthrown because the king puts carrots in their bottom or dicks in their mouth. A kingdom must be overthrown because he is ruling unjustly and hurting his people," said the wizard. "While you were rushing to accomplish a goal that we both shared, I think you were doing it for all the wrong reasons. Your intolerance well-earned your imprisonment. I trust you learned your lesson?"

"I suppose I have," said the man who would soon be a badger again.

"You are lucky I call you friend, mister badger. I am going to let you out of your cage now," said the wizard.

"What of the king? What of the guards? Why would they let

you release me from their castle?" Asked the man who was on the verge of becoming a badger again.

"My friend, the king, is dead. So are all of his guards. Last night I brought an army of werewolves, and they killed everyone," said the wizard. "There are many ways to overthrow a government, but a drunken mob and an audience with the king are not enough. Now an army of bloodthirsty werewolves, that is an effective method of political upheaval!"

"What of the people of the kingdom?" Asked the man who was once a badger.

"Oh, the people who let my friend rot in this cell? Dead," said the wizard. The man who was once a badger felt an immense burden of guilt. It was his fault that the wizard had found out about the werewolves in the first place. He let out a small cry and turned back into a badger.

"They didn't deserve such a fate," said the badger.

"Fate is seldom earned and rarely fair," said the wizard. "If it were not for the werewolves, the result would have been the same. The master I serve seeks an end to all kingdoms. I could have overthrown this little kingdom with the wave of my hand, but these werewolves will serve my master well. I will march these wolves through the mountains into the kingdoms in the north. Do not worry about the politics of man. Go back to your little tree and drink your badger wine."

"The world of man is a chaotic and crazy place. I think I would prefer to live as a badger," he said. The red wizard, Rune, escorted the little badger to the gate in the front of the castle and bid him farewell.

The badger walked through the town on the way back to his tree. The village was still on fire, and there were mangled dead bodies strewn about everywhere. It was a ghastly sight. He shed many tears, but was glad that he was just a badger. He lived a simple badger life for the rest of his days and regretted getting involved with man's politics. It was such a dirty thing, and frankly he was ill suited to be involved.

The End

33

VOID RUNNER

From the Files of Agent Nikita Montauk, Federal Bureau of Investigations Weird Shit Division

Have you ever heard the story of the barn spider and the wasp? No? That's ok.

Barn spiders are smaller and weaker than wasps. Barn spiders don't usually mess with them. It's much easier to eat gnats and flies.

One day a particular barn spider was making his way back to his web. What kind of tasty morsel had he caught this time? The web was shaking violently. As he crawled down his sticky strands, he saw that he had caught a large wasp.

The wasp saw him and stopped moving. It just stared at the spider to see what it would do. The spider mistook this for weakness. Perhaps the wasp had tired out. A big juicy wasp like that could keep a barn spider fed for a while. He had defeated a big bad wasp without even trying.

The spider felt overconfident, so he started talking mad shit to the wasp. He teased, insulted, and laughed. Of course, he wouldn't get too close to the wasp. The spider knew that even tangled in a web, a wasp could still sting. The wasp didn't do anything. It just continued to stare at the spider.

Eventually, the spider became bored of tormenting his prey. He left the web and made his way to the other side of the barn where he had built another web. The spider would come back later, when the wasp would be further tangled, perhaps even dead. Then the little spider could feast.

When the spider returned some hours later, the wasp was gone leaving behind a torn web. It must have struggled free.

The spider was afraid. What if the wasp came back for revenge? He couldn't fight a wasp! He shouldn't have teased the wasp so much!

The wasp never came back, but the spider was uneasy for the rest of his days.

***

I can relate. My name is Nikita Montauk. I am an agent in the FBI Weird Shit Division. I know that sounds exciting. I won't lie, sometimes it is, but most of the time, it's a lot of data entry. You'd think a black book government organization like the FBI-WSD would have streamlined a better system by now, but it hasn't. It's 2083 and I still spend half my time recording mundane reports. I usually arrive at the office as the sun sets. I spend the next two hours with Old Moses.

Back in Bible times, the prophet Moses wrote the first few books of the Old Testament. He recorded the history of humanity up until that point in those chapters. The programmers kept this in mind as they set up the Moses System. Since its set up twenty years ago, every agent needed to report the previous day's events to Old Moses. The system is outdated, but it captures something that a lot of the newer AIs don't. It was programmed to capture context. That's pretty important.

Today, I sat down at my desk, and the little camera interface came down from the ceiling to scan my visor and my cyber suit. All of my data from the previous day's downloads into a harddrive, god knows where. My body temperature, breathing patterns, my com logs, everything I saw, and everything I said are all documented.

That may sound invasive, but honestly, the government sees that and much more for everybody ever since convenience AIs were voluntarily installed in people's homes. It's just not put on the front street like it is for me.

The context comes from my audio reports. AI is smart enough to ask the correct questions, but conclusions still need to be made by humans. At least for now.

I slumped back in my office chair and began my daily interrogation. Last night was particularly uneventful. I sighed deeply as the little computer came out of the ceiling in my office and scanned my visor.

"State your event report for 16:00 to 18:00," Old Moses abruptly commanded in a cold outdated computer voice.

"I patrolled the Northern Quadrant of Cozmos Avenue between 16:00 and 16:23. No significant events. At 16:24 I witnessed a homeless individual urinating in a dumpster. Between 16:25 and 17:03 I patrolled Shine Avenue to follow up on a tip I received about a drug deal. It proved to be a false lead..."

"Expand on this lead," Moses interrupted.

"It was acquired from an anonymous source on the Internet 22 system. It suggested an exchange of red crystal between the Reapers and their supplier in Port Ridge. It was the same tip I described in detail from my report from April 5th."

"Noted. Please continue your report," said the AI

"Between 17:04 and 18:00 I patrolled Quadrant B of Highway 54. No significant events," I said.

"Visor systems support your event report as 78% accurate. State your event report for 18:00 to 20:00," Old Moses demanded. It went on like this until every minute of the previous night was accounted for. Finally, it was time to leave the office and head out on patrol. That's when I'm really in my element. When I'm out in the streets at night where anything can happen and the weirdness sets in, I'm at the top of my game.

It was January and the first snow of the year was coming down pretty hard. I remember thinking that it might be the last time snow would fall on Saint Croix. As you may have seen, dome cities are becoming all the rage these days. Central City had been domed just three years earlier, and they were enjoying the perfection of artificial weather. Angel City was also being domed, but the project there was experiencing workforce issues, and there have been numerous delays. I chalked it up to the sluggishness of bureaucracy. Projects fall behind all the time. I didn't give it much thought.

Then there was an incident in the heart of the east dome construction site right here in Saint Croix. They found a body. I read the autopsy report when it came in. There was no entry wound, but there was a two-inch cut in the left ventricle of the victim's heart. Internal bleeding did him in. It was a clean-cut like a knife wound, but again, no broken skin. The coroners couldn't explain it. It was odd, but I let it go. I'm no doctor.

I didn't start really investigating until a few nights later when they found another body at the north dome construction site. It had the same unexplained cause of death. I visited the site to check it out and see for myself. The construction team worked at night. I saw nothing. There was no evidence of a fight or a struggle. The workers there told me that the same thing happened in Angel City. I had to dig deeper.

"Old Moses, please pull up all event reports regarding the Angel City dome construction sites. Send them to my visor," I said aloud to the ever present AI.

"Transfer complete," it replied into my earpiece.

Cyberskin or not, it was cold out there in the snow. I ducked into a nearby Fuckin' Donuts and read the files. The project to dome Angel City wasn't just behind, it was suspended indefinitely. There were bodies there too, but there was also an obvious cover-up. The police had records of the first three bodies, but not the next five. Those only existed on Old Moses in event reports made by an Agent Dustin Riverhead.

"Old Moses, please pull up Agent Dustin Riverhead's schedule for today," I commanded.

"He works from 19:00 - 04:00 this evening," it said.

"Please open Visor Chat," I continued.

"You have three new messages," said Old Moses.

"Ignore. Open a connection to Agent Dustin Riverhead," I said.

"Please stand by as I connect you…"

There was a long pause while I waited. Riverhead was probably sizing me up. Maybe he was skimming my files on the database before responding? I wouldn't blame him if he was. I would have done the same thing. Being in this line of work teaches you to be cautious. I nursed my cup of coffee as I waited.

"This is Agent Riverhead," he finally said as the channel opened.

"Good evening Agent Riverhead, I am Agent Nikita Montauk from the WSD in Saint Croix. I was hoping I could speak with you about the Void Runner case," I stated. I heard him exhale heavily before he responded.

"That's a pretty complex case," he said.

"I've already gone over the event reports. A couple of bodies have been found here and I'm seeing many similarities to what happened in Angel City last year," I said.

"Ok, we've got plenty to go over then. Come down to the Angel City office tomorrow, and we'll go over it in detail. Is 20:00 ok?" He asked.

"That's fine," I said.

"Great. I'll see you then," he said before cutting off the channel. I made the arrangements with Old Moses.

The next afternoon I was on the bullet train to Angel City. A 300 mile trip in just under an hour. I know it's slow compared to Photon Travel, but I enjoy the concept of a journey. Call me sentimental.

I checked into the WSD office in Angel City and met with Riverhead. He suggested we get dinner and talk there. I'm not stupid. It was obvious he was trying to turn our meeting into a date. I could tell by the way he looked at me, but as long as he told me what I needed to know, I could handle him. He took me to TGIN Mondays. Classy. He was a little taller than me and very muscular. I could tell he had some augments in his legs by the way he walked. His stride was powerful, but lacked grace. That's always the trade-off with augs. I'm sure he could jump three stories high with those legs, but he's not sneaking up on anybody the way he clomped around. Still, he was handsome and would make a good catch if I was interested in such things. I didn't have patients for this little roleplay, so as soon as we sat down, I went right into it.

"So who is the Void Runner?" I asked.

"You don't waste time, do you? The Void Runner is a teenage girl. She's Asian. I haven't been able to identify her further than that," he said. I frowned. He better not have dragged me all the way out here for this.

"Has your visor captured any images?" I asked.

"Just this blurry one," he said. "I'm sending it to you now." An out of focus image popped up on my visor. Just as he said, the Void Runner looked young. If she was a teenager, then she could not be more than thirteen or fourteen in the image. She was wearing a black hoodie and had purple hair. It wasn't much to go by. I change my hair color up every few weeks or so. This image was a couple of years old. With a girl this young, her appearance could have changed drastically since then.

"How do you know it was her aside from you catching her at the scene of the crime twice? I don't even understand how she did it," I admitted. As I said this, the waitress approached our table.

"Hello! My name is Monica, and I'll be your server today. Can I start you off with some drinks?" she asked.

"I'll have a scotch and the lady will have a glass of your finest wine," said Riverhead. I shook my head. Were we doing this, really? The waitress and I shared a glance. She probably saw this kind of thing all the time.

"The lady will have a glass of Fizz Cola, thanks," I said. The waitress nodded.

"Ok, I'll be right back with that," said Monica as she tucked her tablet back into her apron and left.

"Little Miss doesn't drink eh?" he said with a raised eyebrow. I screamed internally, but maintained my composure.

"Business before pleasure. I'm on the clock Agent Riverhead. I came here for information. Tell me everything you know about the Void Runner," I said. He seemed to have taken the hint.

"Alrighty then, are you familiar with the concept of the Twisting Nether?" He asked. I was.

"Yeah. The Twisting Nether was mentioned in the recordings left by the time travelers. It's a void that magic energy can be drawn from," I recounted.

"She mentioned it in one of our encounters. Then she just vanished," he explained.

"Like a succubus?" I asked.

"Maybe," said Riverhead. "The only succubi that teleport are the ones in Saint Croix. I've never seen one that could do it."

"Sorry, I forgot that only ours could do that," I said. "I'll check into it."

"We have a wizard living in Angel City. I talked to him and he said that he never heard of a spell that can cut a man's heart from the inside," he said.

"Do we have a motive?" I asked.

"I never figured it out. The bodies piled up. The dome project was suspended, the killings stopped, and the trail went cold," he said. "I hadn't heard anything until you contacted me last night."

"You said she mentioned the Twisting Nether. In what context was that?" I asked.

Riverhead stared at me, then he blinked five times and bit his lower lip. I understood and turned off the data connection on my visor. He did the same. It was a code that the higher-ups had not caught onto yet. If two agents needed to talk off the record we could turn off our visors for five minutes before any red flags were raised in the system. This was allowed for privacy reasons, so the government didn't record us using the restroom.

"Thank you for disconnecting. I know it will affect your percentages. The truth is, I noticed a lot of the higher-ups logging into and altering my reports. There's something weird about this one, so I kept my reports vague," he explained.

"I've seen the top brass snooping around in a few of my cases too. I understand," I assured him.

"I have video of the encounter, but it was never loaded to

Old Moses. I switched off my visor connection and stored it on a data card. I'm going to show it to you. It's pretty quick. We'll talk for a minute, but then we have to turn our connections back on and you need to act like you just got back from the bathroom," he explained.

"Ok, I know the drill," I said. "Show me the footage."

A video from the point of view of Riverhead started playing on my visor. It was dark and a little out of focus, but I could still make everything out. In the distance the body of a construction worker sat sprawled and lifeless on the ground. Riverhead began to walk toward it when there was the sound of footsteps to his right. He turned, and a teenage girl in a black hoodie walked out from an alley. It was a little hard to make out. When the girl noticed Riverhead she stopped dead in her tracks, and her eyes went wide. Riverhead didn't hesitate.

"I know you're killing these men. Why are you doing it?" He asked before she could compose herself. She blinked and swallowed.

"Who the fuck are you?" she asked. "You're just a bug compared to the Twisting Nether."

"The what?" Riverhead yelled, but it was too late. She vanished. Well, she didn't exactly vanish. It was as if she fell into the floor. Like there was a trapdoor that opened beneath her feet. Riverhead looked down, but there was only hard concrete where she stood. The video ended.

"I spent the next thirty minutes searching the area to see where she went, but I found nothing," he told me as I closed out the video and deleted the file. "Then the cops showed up to bag the body."

"Did you ever find a connection between the dome and the Twisting Nether?" I asked.

"No," he said. Then time was up and our visors connected to the network. "Ah, you're back. You were in the bathroom for a while. Are you ok?"

"Must have been something I ate," I answered. I asked him some general questions about the case to avoid suspicion and then I was on my way, back on the bullet train riding to St. Croix. My mind was racing the whole way.

For the next few days, I was on a succubus hunt. It was all I had to go on. We know the places they frequent, but not where they live. The truth is, we don't go after the succubi even though they kill people. If we did, we couldn't hold them. They could just teleport out. We can't kill them because they are immortal. I tried to meet with Anastasia. She was the one that everyone called The Vampire Queen even though she wasn't a vampire. It's a long story. In short, she is a succubus and she found herself leading the vampires in the city after their last leader caught a wooden stake in his chest. The whole thing turned out to be a dead end. The bloodsuckers just laughed at me, and my audience was denied.

There was another succubus in the city named Brandy, and she was much easier to find. Brandy had been seducing the men in this town for over 70 years. I contacted her in one of the chat forums on the Internet 22 system. We met on the roof of an apartment complex downtown. I had been waiting for about ten minutes when she teleported in.

"Brandy, we meet again," I said when I noticed her.

"What can I do for you, officer?" She asked. I could tell she didn't want to talk to me. The Weird Shit Division and the Succubi had a mutual respect, but that didn't mean we liked each other.

"Bodies are starting to pile up at the dome construction site," I said.

"I fail to see what I have to do with that," she said.

"The killer can teleport," I said.

"Well, I can see why you would want to talk to me about this, but I still have nothing to do with it. Have you spoken to her majesty?" She asked. Brandy put air up quotes when she said her majesty. It seems Brandy and Anastasia were no longer on good terms.

"No, I haven't," I answered. "I don't suspect any succubi. The dead bodies don't fit your methods. Its more of a fact-finding meeting."

"Flaccid dicks huh? What do you want?" Brandy asked. I could tell she was relieved that she was no longer in danger of being accused.

"Tell me what you know about the Twisting Nether," I said.

"Rune mentioned it from time to time. It's a chaos dimension he pulled magic from," Brandy said.

"Do you use it to teleport?" I asked.

"No, we pull from a different void powered by souls. It's more shamanistic than Twisting Nether stuff," she said.

"Could you use your teleportation to cut a man's heart while it's still in his body?" I asked.

"What? No. That doesn't even make sense," she said.

"Where's Rune now?" I asked.

"Rune is gone. You won't find him," said Brandy. There was a short silence. I could tell I just asked something I wasn't supposed to ask. I decided to just drop it.

"Ok... thanks, Brandy," I said. I started climbing down the fire escape.

"Whatever," said Brandy before she teleported out.

It was a dead-end, and I was all out of options. All I could do was stalk the construction site and try to play defense against something I didn't understand. I spent the next two weeks traveling from site to site, waiting for something to happen. There were no bodies either. I was starting to think that would be the end of it. It would be another mystery. Then another blizzard hit.

A body was found on the northside of town. I was two blocks away when it was called in. I ran through the blizzard, hoping to catch a glimpse of the killer. The victim's body was sprawled out on the snow face down. There was no need for a chalk outline this time. His form was preserved as an imprint in the snow like a morbid snow angel.

I scanned the area looking for footprints in the snow or some kind of clue as to where the killer had gone. There were no footprints, but I did come across a place where there was no snow. I filed this away as I noticed a warehouse nearby. In my experience, there are two things a killer can do after a murder. They could flee the scene of the crime or they could stay and watch everything unfold. If she fled, then she's gone. That would be that, but if she was the type to stay, the warehouse would be the place to watch.

I ran around the back so she wouldn't see me coming. The place seemed empty, but the lights were on. I crouched behind a box and I saw a pile of melting snow. Then it all made sense. The Void Runner couldn't teleport. She created portals. The melting snow in the warehouse was the snow missing from outside. Wet footprints were leading toward the elevator. I took the stairs and I found her staring out a window overlooking the crime scene. She turned around as I drew my gun.

"You killed that man out there, didn't you?" I asked. She didn't say anything. This purple haired teenager just looked at me. "Why did you do it?" I asked. I knew she was about to run, and I needed to stall her.

"I did it becau…," she started. I shot her with a tranquilizer. I wasn't about to let her get away, and there would be plenty of time for her to talk in one of our holding cells. My visor did capture her confession. She dropped to the floor immediately. I called it in.

We got her to the station and kept her heavily sedated. She couldn't open a portal now. I didn't know much about the Twisting Nether, but I was willing to bet that drawing from it requires a great deal of concentration. With the stuff she was on, that wasn't going to happen. Drugging a prisoner against their will isn't exactly legal, but the WSD doesn't officially exist either, so we usually don't worry about it.

A few hours later, she was restrained and sitting across the table from me in the interrogation room. The Void Runner was not happy.

"Ok, now where were we?" I asked.

"You bitch! What did you do to me?!" She yelled.

"We had to give you a mild sedative to calm your nerves

and…"

"…Sap my powers?" She interrupted.

"Sap your powers? Yes. We can't have you running off now. We have so much to talk about," I said. "We've identified you based on retinal scans as Casandra Cho age 19 from Angel City. I was just there a week ago. Weather is nice there in the spring."

"You can thank me for that," she said.

"So it's safe to say that you were killing construction workers to stop the dome projects?" I asked.

"Yeah," she said.

"That's two recorded confessions from you tonight. You're doing good Casandra. Now I know you weren't doing it because of the weather. That would be crazy. You aren't crazy are you?" I asked.

"No. Damn, you're a bitch," she said. I smiled.

"Then, why?" I asked.

"It was the Twisting Nether. There is something in there. It told me that the glass negates its power," she said. Little Casandra was becoming frantic now. Beads of sweat formed on her forehead and streaked down her face. I pressed on.

"How can something exist in the nether? It's pure chaos," I asked.

"I can. It's how I teleport. I enter the nether and use it as the line between two points. Why am I telling you this?" She asked.

"Why indeed? It could be the drugs. Please go on. Are there more living things in the nether?" I continued. I had her, this little bird was going to tell me everything.

"Just me and him," she answered.

"Who is he?" I asked. I leaned forward.

"The most powerful being we'll probably ever see. He came to me in a dream and gave me my powers. Told me to stop the domes," she said.

"And you were happy to do it. Like a good little minion," I asserted.

"What do you want from me?" She asked.

"I'd like to speak with him," I answered. The Void Runner

let out a pained laugh. It started as a chuckle at first, but it became louder and more boisterous. Tears swelled in the corners of her eyes and mixed with the sweat cascading down her face. I was taken aback.

"What's so funny?" I asked. I was losing control of the conversation and didn't like it.

"I'm sorry," she said in between bursts of laughter, "but why would he want to talk to a piss ant like you?"

"I think it's time for you to go to your cell," I said as I motioned to the doctors on the other side of the interrogation glass. Two large men came into the room and held her down as I injected her with another sedative. Casandra kept laughing until she passed out.

I wish I had continued because the next day, she vanished from her cell. I've watched the security tapes. She was injected with a sedative an hour before she disappeared. She shouldn't have been able to summon the nether while she was drugged, but she did.

It took me a while, but I think I figured that part out. She killed her victims by opening a small portal inside their heart, then piercing it with a knife from within the void. This makes her the deadliest opponent I've ever faced. I can't defend against that. If we meet again I don't think she would hesitate to kill me.

She did something similar to escape. She may not have been able to concentrate enough to open a portal big enough for her to escape, but what if she opened up a small portal in her vein? The sedative we injected would flow right into the void. She must have waited for the effects to wear off and then just left. I may never find out for sure.

The dome project was canceled a week later. The "accidents" must have been getting too hard to cover up. Void Runner is still out there, but the killings ended when the project was canned.

I don't do what I do for a sense of justice. I do it to find out the truth. I didn't solve the puzzle this time, but I connected quite a few pieces. My work is saved on Old Moses. I check this file now and then to see if there are any new pieces. So far there aren't. I've felt uneasy ever since.

THE END

ATLANTIC CITY KAIJU

The ancient thing slept under the salty waves that carried the garbage to and fro. It slept beneath the sand and rocks that housed the little fish that sharks munched on in the dark watery void. The sun didn't reach the depths of this murky sea, but the ancient thing was warm and comfortable. The heat from the earth's core caressed its belly keeping the beast relaxed. It slept.

A while back, the ancient thing awakened. The Christ man finally died up on that cross and the earth shook with God's fury. The thing woke up and ascended to the surface. It basked in the sun and swam until it was tired. After taking a deep breath, it sunk back down below the surface and covered itself with mud, sand, and rocks. There it slept until something disturbed it again. This time it wasn't the death of God's son, but something equally significant. It was July 15th 1998, and Hello Nasty by The Beastie Boys was released.

***

Directly above the ancient thing, Todd and Josh were sat in an 18-foot fishing boat that belonged to Josh's father. They had just graduated high school and the two of them were spending their summer fluke fishing on the south side of Long Island. Josh was having a good day. He caught a sea bass and a 22-inch fluke. Todd, on the other hand, caught nothing but sea robins.

Sea robins are a bottom-feeding garbage fish that taste so bad that they aren't worth cooking. If you caught one, your best bet is to grab it by its toothless bottom lip, pull the hook out, and throw it back so it could waste someone else's time. They are synonymous with disappointment when fishing in the northeast.

"Well, I'm just fucked today," Todd cursed as he tried freeing the hook from his fourth sea robin. The hook was lodged tight back there. "I'm so sick of these ugly bastards." Josh just ignored him and stared at the bay. Todd's fingers were now a full inch down the fish's throat. It croaked and spread out its wing like fins as Todd started jerking at the hook.

"It's still early," said Josh trying to instill a little hope in his friend. Todd got fed up and ripped the hook out of the sea robin's throat. Some guts spilled out with it. He threw the fish back in the water and baited his hook. The sinker made a blooping sound as he let down his line again to restart the process.

"I came out here to catch Bubba," Todd sighed. Bubba is a legendary fluke that the fishermen on Long Island like to joke about catching. He's the big one that got away. "All I can catch are these damn sea robins. It's so god damn disappointing! I haven't been this disappointed since Seinfeld ended a couple of months ago."

"Here we go," Josh said under his breath.

"God damn! You spend the last nine years watching the best show ever and even though it's not as good as it used to be, you figure it'll end on a high note. Larry David even comes back to write the final episode! It's all over the news! The whole cast is on the cover of Rolling Stone. Then after all that build up, what do we get? A two part clips episode with a stupid plot that makes you feel like bashing your head on a brick wall. Now after I suffer through all that hype and disappointment, I'm like it's ok. There's a new Godzilla movie coming out and Ferris Bueller is in it! Fuck yeah! So a week later I watch it and it's absolute garbage! That is not Godzilla! Hollywood really fucked that one up! Do I let that get me down, though? Nah, it's cool. My buddy Josh and I are going to spend the summer fluke fishing. I'm determined to catch Bubba, and everything is going to be cool before we go off to college. We're going to make the most of it. Nope! It's obvious that I'm going to spend the summer ripping the guts out of sea robins! Fuck!"

"At least the new Beastie Boys album is good though," Josh

said, trying to lighten the mood.

"Fuck yeah it is! You want another Coke?" asked Todd.

"Yeah, sounds good," said Josh. Todd got up and put his pole in the rod holder. He opened the cooler and grabbed two cans of Coke, and handed one to Josh as he popped the tab on his own. He unzipped his pants, pulled out his dick, and started pissing off the side of the boat.

"I guess I should try and be more positive. The Knicks are in the finals and Game 1 is tomorrow." said Todd as he peed. Then while still peeing, he downed the Coke with his free hand. You have to replace your liquids after all. When he was done, he pulled the CD boombox out of the cabin and started playing Hello Nasty by the Beastie Boys. He skipped to Intergalactic.

"INTERGALACTIC PLANETARY PLANETARY INTERGAL-ACTIC," a computer voice began to sing. "INTERGALACTIC PLANETARY PLANETARY INTERGALACTIC ANOTHER DIMEN-SION ANOTHER DIMENSION ANOTHER DIMENSION ANOTHER DIMENSION" As the computer voice droned on the octave went lower and lower until it resembled the sound of a frog croaking. The sound traveled down through the dirty water down to the mud and sand where the ancient thing slept.

The ancient thing opened its eyes. What was this croaking noise? Was this a mate? Hell yeah! Its animal urges surpassed the beast's laziness, and it began to swim upward to find its mate. Within seconds its large protruding gold eyes broke the surface of the water. It stared at the little fishing boat.

"What the fuck is that!?" Josh yelled.

"Holy shit!" Yelled Todd. "It looks like a giant sea robin! It's huge!" Without thinking, he pushed pause on the boombox, and the music stopped.

"He's probably pissed that you keep gutting his children," said Josh.

"Dude, how are you even making jokes right now?! Stand still and don't move. Maybe it won't see us." said Todd in the calm-est voice he could muster.

"This isn't Jurassic Park," Josh said.

The ancient thing honestly looked more like a frog than a sea robin. It could see them and ultimately found Todd and Josh pretty disappointing. Just like their parents. It became bored, belched, vomited a little, and began swimming south. It swam off into the distance until they couldn't see it anymore. Todd and Josh sat in silence for a while.

"Welp, we saw Bubba Sea Robin. Let's go home," said Josh.

"Yep," said Todd and they left.

***

They called him Robbie the Fist and he lived in the Taj Mahal in Atlantic City. It wasn't cheap to live in the casino, and Robbie wasn't a high roller, but the people who employed him were wealthy. They needed him close and would call him at any time to fulfill his duties. He specialized in collecting money owed from desperate people who needed cash, borrowed money, and were late paying it back. To be good at a job like this, one only needed a hammer and a keen disposition for brutality. Robbie had both, but he rarely used the hammer. He had the stature of a mountain that religiously went to the gym after drinking raw eggs for breakfast. His bare fists were the only hammers that he used most nights.

He was needed tonight. Robbie was a light sleeper, and as soon as the telephone rang, he was sitting on the edge of his bed, answering the call on the second ring.

"This is Robbie," he said into the receiver. He wiped the sleep from his eyes with his free hand.

"Robbie, I need you to collect for me tonight," said the voice on the other line. The voice sounded like wet gravel from a dirty fish tank pouring into a kitchen sink. It was Shark Daddy. He was one of the many loan sharks that made his living feeding on the desperation that a town like Atlantic City attracted.

"Which casino?" Robbie asked.

"Showboat," said Shark Daddy.

"Right. I'll be there in twenty minutes," he said.

"Better make it fifteen. I'm not sure how long our guy will be here," said Shark. There was a click as Shark hung up the phone.

Robbie lit a cigarette and looked at the clock. It was 4:36 am. The night was no longer young. It was an awkward 33-year-old with a drinking problem. After his second drag, Robbie stood up and quickly got dressed before walking through the door into the gaudy hotel hallway.

He walked past the gaming tables with the waitresses dressed like genies serving drinks to middle aged men playing blackjack with dirty Taj Mahal chips, past the restaurants and gift shops that sold neon orange shirts and decks of blue Taj Mahal cards with a hole punched through the center so they couldn't be used at the tables. Then he walked into the second-floor hallway that went over the street and connected the two casinos.

The Showboat Casino was a different monster all together. In Showboat it was an eternal Mardi Gras. Robbie didn't bother to take in the sights. He walked through the lobby and opened a maintenance door. The hallways behind this Cajun farce were much less colorful. After a few twists and turns, he scanned his key card and ascended an elevator and made his way to the security control room.

When he entered, the room was full of cigarette smoke. A team of security guards lounged about casually watching monitors of the gambling guests.

"Hey Robbie, how have you been?" Asked one of the guards as he stirred up a fresh cup of instant coffee. "Are you working tonight?"

"I'm about to be. Where's Shark Daddy?" He asked.

"He's over there," said the guard pointing to the far side of the room.

"How's his mood?" Asked Robbie.

"Oh, you know, Shark Daddy. He's all sunshine and blow-jobs," laughed the guard. Robbie patted the guard on the shoulder and made his way across the room. He passed two islands of monitors and descended a little stairway and found Shark Daddy lounging at a station with his feet on the desk.

Shark Daddy was an older man in his mid-50s. He wore a white suit with a brown fedora. In one hand he held a glass of scotch. The other hand lazily flicked the ash from his cigar onto the floor. When Robbie sat down next to him, Shark Daddy didn't take his eyes off the monitor.

"Hey Robbie, thank you for being prompt. This is why you were the employee of the month," said Shark Daddy. Robbie didn't even know if Shark Daddy had any other employees. He had never met any of them. He was the employee of the month every month it seemed. This prestigious title earned him the luxurious gift certificate for a free slice of pizza at the little Italian restaurant on the boardwalk. Robbie never asked unnecessary questions. He enjoyed his private pizza party every month and left it at that.

"So, what are we looking at, boss?" Asked Robbie. Shark Daddy pointed at the monitor.

"You see this guy at the blackjack table in the light blue dress shirt? That's Baltimore Cherry. He owes me 7k. He's having a good night and if he cashes out now, we can collect. He's probably going to fuck this up soon, so I need you down there asap," said Shark Daddy.

"Ok boss, I'm on it," said Robbie as he stood up. Shark Daddy looked up at him.

"Be careful with this guy. He's slippery," said Shark Daddy. Robbie nodded and quickly climbed up the stairs.

Baltimore Cherry was a regular at the Showboat casino hotel. He lived in a modest apartment five blocks away from the boardwalk. By day he worked at a convenience store called Beer and Cigs. By night he was a terrible gambler pissing his money away at the blackjack tables.

Six months back, he couldn't afford his rent, so he took out a loan from Shark Daddy. This pattern continued for a few months, and now he was in the hole for 7k. The plan was for him to pay his rent and take a little extra for gambling purposes.

Tonight, he was up 8k. This wasn't because of skill. Baltimore wasn't good enough at math to count cards. It wasn't because he was cheating. Tonight, it was just blind luck. It started when he walked into the casino and found out that he had won an hourly drawing for $250 in match play. He got lucky on some side bets and things just snowballed.

When he felt a tap on his shoulder he hoped it was a beautiful woman who had taken notice. It was that kind of night. At least, it could have been. Instead he turned and saw Robbie towering over him.

"Hey man, what's up?" Baltimore asked. He was caught off guard.

"I work for Shark Daddy. Finish up this hand, then you and I will take a little walk," said Robbie.

"No, no, no, not now! I'm on a roll. I'm on the verge of some Scrooge McDuck shit right now! I got enough to make some big plays!" Baltimore said.

"Shark Daddy wants his money. Luck is on your side. You can pay him and get him off your back," said Robbie. "Come with me and we can cash out your chips." Baltimore let out a long sigh. His magical night was about to end abruptly.

"Ok, last hand," he said holding up his index finger. He busted and lost $50.

"Put your chips in the bag. Let's go," said Robbie. Baltimore put his chips in a velvet bag with the Showboat logo on it. "Good, now let's take a little walk so we can cash you out."

***

Baltimore was not a smart man and his plan to escape this situation wasn't very clever. It did work out in his favor at the end, but the events that led him were unforeseen by all parties involved.

Step 1 was probably the worst idea in the bunch. The two men walked to the desk and cashed out all the chips. When Baltimore started counting the money he looked off into the distance and was stunned.

"Is that Trent Reznor?" He said while squinting.

"Oh shit, really?" Asked Robbie while turning around gazing at the crowd. He didn't see him. Robbie turned back toward Baltimore and caught a sucker punch in the face.

Robbie is a tough motherfucker, but he can be caught off guard just like anyone else. He wasn't knocked out cold, but he did instinctively grab his face and stumble backwards. Baltimore wasn't much of a fighter and the punch didn't even hurt that much. It just surprised Robbie that this even happened.

Step 2 of Baltimore's plan was more sensible considering the circumstances. Run like hell. Baltimore flew through the lobby with his fist tightly clenching the fat stack of cash. He didn't have time to pocket it. He just ran towards the back of the casino.

Robbie regained his composure and began to give chase. In the back of his mind he hoped that Shark Daddy didn't see him get punched on camera. He shook off the thought. The only thing that mattered now was catching up to Baltimore and collecting that money. Robbie was bigger and stronger, but Baltimore was fast. It took everything Robbie had to keep up with him.

Baltimore hit the door that led to the boardwalk hard and ran out into the night. Seconds later, Robbie was outside trying to figure out which way he went. He was about to give up when he saw a twenty-dollar bill to his right, just sitting on the ground. Baltimore must have run south toward the Taj Mahal. Robbie bolted down the wooden street, hoping he could salvage this failure of a night.

Baltimore Cherry was hiding behind a particularly gaudy cement statue of an elephant that rested on a square pillar at the foot of a staircase leading into the second floor of the Taj Mahal. The elephant itself was painted white and it was decorated with a cloth that draped over its back. The fabric was painted to show gold ropes dangling down to the animal's feet, but the gold paint was old and chipping.

Cherry tried to stuff all the money into his pants pocket, but his hands were sweaty and he was out of breath. It took him a minute to get some air into his lungs. Just as he did, he saw Robbie run past him. Baltimore Cherry went wide eyed. The money was sticking to his sweaty palms. He dared not pull his hand out of his pocket for fear that all the cash would fly out and scatter all over the boardwalk. In panic, he ran out of his now-defunct hiding spot and made a beeline for The Steel Pier with one hand in his pocket still.

(Think of a really good Alanis Morissette joke and put it here. It will be really funny and maybe a girl with a good sense of humor might put your penis in their mouth.)

The sound of Baltimore's running on the wooden planks was much louder than he expected. Robbie may have been a good twenty yards ahead, but he still heard Baltimore clomping towards the pier. He skidded to a stop and turned around just in time to see Baltimore disappear behind the large archway that led to The Steel Pier.

For those of you who have never been to Atlantic City, The Steel Pier is an amusement park built on top of a concrete pier that juts out into the ocean behind the Taj Mahal. The pier used to have steel supports holding it above the water, but back in 1904, a portion of it was washed away. It was rebuilt with concrete supports and still operates to this day. It's a modest park with go-karts, a ferris wheel, carnival games, and a roller coaster.

Baltimore Cherry ran past the closed shops in the dark tunnel that led to the pier. He was hopeful that he could hide in the closed park until Robbie gave up the chase. That thought soon faded when he heard, "Get back here, you stupid son of a bitch!!!" It was Robbie yelling at him from behind.

"Fuck you and fuck Shark Daddy!" Yelled Baltimore as he ran. Robbie barely heard him. It sounded like unintelligible screaming to him. Robbie was focused - he wasn't letting this one get away, especially after that sucker punch. It didn't even make sense that Baltimore was running away. Everything would be so much easier for everyone involved if he would just pay up.

This was around the time Baltimore got his hand out of his pocket. Miraculously, all the money stayed in his pants. At the end of the tunnel he made a sharp right and zigzagged through some carnival booths trying to get out of Robbie's sight. It worked.

When Robbie exited the dark tunnel into the deserted amusement park Baltimore was nowhere to be seen. Baltimore continued to run until he reached the ferris wheel. He ducked down behind the elevated platform, catching his breath.

Now he just needed to wait and sneak his way off the pier. Then he would be free to get to the airport and skip town. He could start somewhere new. Maybe Las Vegas. That would be a good start. At least, he thought so. Baltimore Cherry caught his breath and began to observe his surroundings. There was a go-kart track a little further up the pier. That wouldn't help much. There were plenty of carnival booths to hide behind. That could be advantageous. There was also a giant frog climbing onto the roller coaster. That was...probably bad.

Robbie screamed when he saw the giant frog making its way onto the pier. It was almost as big as the ferris wheel. The ancient one let out a deep croak that made the ground vibrate. Robbie lost his balance and landed on his ass.

The ancient one looked toward the city. There was something about the bright casino lights that caught its attention. It hopped forward with a force that caused part of the pier to collapse and landed on the archway that led back to the boardwalk. The tunnel caved in under the beast's weight. Robbie and Baltimore were trapped.

Robbie ran toward the back of the pier to get away from the monstrous amphibian. When he reached the end of the pier, he saw Baltimore looking forward in shock.

"What the fuck is that thing?" He asked half in a trance. Neither one of them cared about the money anymore.

"I don't fucking know, and I don't fucking care," said Robbie. "We have to get the fuck off this pier."

The ancient one let out another deep croak. The pier started to shake again. The ground beneath them began to crack.

"This whole damn pier is going to collapse!" Baltimore

said. Robbie took off his shoes.

"I'm going to jump off the side and swim to shore. I'm not getting stuck under any rubble," Robbie said. Baltimore took off his shoes too. Both men silently walked up to the flattened chain link fence where the monster had climbed originally. They looked down. It was a long fall.

"How deep do you think it is?" Asked Baltimore. Another croak. The ground shook more violently this time.

"Guess we'll find out soon enough," Robbie said as he dived in. Baltimore took another look at the frog. It hadn't moved. He took a deep breath and jumped.

The monstrous frog jumped again, and as it did, half of the pier collapsed into the cold New Jersey water. The ancient one was now perched on top of the Taj Mahal. The building creaked and shook, but maintained its integrity. The frog sat there and watched the sun rise. People started to evacuate the area soon after. To the frog, they looked like little ants running in all directions. The frog's tongue darted out of its mouth and snatched a few people from the chaos and swallowed them whole. They tasted greasy, but satisfying. It happened again and again. Most people did manage to escape, but when the chaos settled, sixty-four people had been eaten. One of the unlucky snacks was Shark Daddy. Eventually, the only ant left within range of the ancient thing was the owner of the casino. It was Donald Trump.

"Get down from there you toad bastard!" Donald yelled at the giant frog. "How dare this thing sit atop my beautiful casino! It's the nicest casino in Atlantic City! Lots of people are saying so! It's the best! Now, go away!"

The frog ate him, he tasted gross. That was the end of Donald Trump! He certainly didn't become president of the United States or anything. That would be ridiculous.

It was around this time when the ancient one began to urinate. A waterfall of two-thousand-year-old urine ran down the tower's side. Under normal circumstances people would say that the smell was awful, but since this happened in New Jersey, no one noticed.

(Just kidding New Jersey. Relax.)

The fighter jets that the military sent showed up around 7 am. They flew at the monster and shot high caliber bullets and missiles at it. The creature was annoyed, but it didn't move from it's spot. At one point the frog snatched one of the jets out of the sky with it's fast sticky tongue. It exploded in it's mouth and injured the creature. Only then did it jump back into the sea. It hasn't been seen since. The media referred to the monster as King Slippy because that's what a high ranking government third grader was calling it in the military war room. He has since been promoted to fourth grade because of his service to our country and because summer vacation is over.

***

Robbie and Baltimore washed ashore during the evacuation. Neither of them cared about the money anymore. They parted ways at the boardwalk and never saw or heard from each other again. After Robbie learned about Shark Daddy's death, he took his savings and moved to Colorado. The ocean is filled with weird and deadly things. He got as far away from it as possible. Baltimore still lives in Atlantic City, but gave up gambling. He owns an ABC Liquor store on Pacific Avenue.

END

YEAH

The courtroom was completely silent except for the shuffling of papers. Katarina Tillman had her eyes locked on the witness. It was once again her turn to question him. She was tall and fit and had a sharp mind. Her quick wit served her well as a prosecutor. She stood up and began walking toward the witness.

The witness was a twenty-seven year old construction worker named Carson Ross. The side of his mouth twitched as she approached. He was nervous. This was the first time he had ever been in a courtroom. Katarina could smell the blood in the water.

"Mister Ross, in your statement you said that you had gone out drinking on the night in question. Is that correct?" She began.

"Yes, that's correct," he replied.

"What were you drinking?"

"Fish bowls," he said.

"Mister Ross, I may not look it, but I know how to party. I know what a fish bowl is, but for the record, can you state what that drink entails?" She asked with a faint smirk.

"Yeah, it's rum and fruit juice mixed up in a fish bowl full of ice," he said.

"It usually comes with a of couple straws. Were you sharing it with anyone?" Katerina asked.

"No, I nursed it myself," he stated.

"How many fish bowls did you drink that night?" she asked.

"Objection your honor!" Shouted the defense attorney. "The witness knows how to party. I don't think it is necessary to gauge his crunkness based on the amount of fish bowls he can kick back."

"Your honor, the witness's credibility as a righteous party animal, is pivotal to the motive of the defendant. I'm simply trying to paint a vivid picture of the night in question," said Katerina.

"I'll allow it," said the judge. "Please proceed."

"I drank three fish bowls," said Carson.

"Damn, son!" said Katarina. "You must have been drunk as hell!"

"I was, yes," said Carson.

"Tight. Now there was also karaoke at the bar. Is that correct?" Asked Katarina.

"Yes, there was," said Carson.

"Did you go up and sing anything?" Asked Katrina.

"I did. I sang 'Plush' by The Stone Temple Pilots," said Carson.

"That's a good one," said Katarina. "I also heard you did 'Rollin' by Limp Bizkit. Is that true?"

"I vaguely remember that. I was pretty drunk." said Carson. The courtroom audibly gasped.

"Are you a fan of Limp Bizkit?" Asked Katarina.

"No. I just did it as a joke," said Carson.

"I remind you that you are under oath. Now I'm going to ask you one more time. Are you a fan of Limp Bizkit?" asked Katarina.

"Objection your honor!" cried the defense attorney. "The witness is not on trial! He does not need to incriminate himself by admitting that he likes Limp Bizkit."

"Katarina, I'm going to let you continue. Don't make me regret it," said the judge.

"Mister Ross, are you a fan of Limp Bizkit?" Katarina asked again.

"I am not," said Carson.

"I would like to introduce exhibit A. This is a signed copy of Chocolate Starfish and the Hot Dog Flavored Water signed by Fred Durst. It reads 'Carson Ross 233-65-2312, Keep on rockin Baby!'. Is that number in Fred's handwriting your social security number?" Asked Katarina.

"Yes, it is," admitted Carson.

"So, this is your copy of Chocolate Starfish and the Hot Dog Flavored Water?" Asked Katarina.

"I mean, yeah, I guess it is," said Carson.

"Why did you have Fred Durst write your social security number on it?" Asked Katarina.

"I don't know. I just thought it'd be funny." said Carson.

"I would like to introduce exhibit B. This is a picture of Carson's penis. It has the phrase 'Keep on Rollin Rollin Rollin' tattooed on it. Did you have Limp Bizkit lyrics tattooed on your penis because you thought it would be funny too?"

"Yes, I did," said Carson.

"Carson. You clearly like Limp Bizkit," said Katarina. "The prosecution rests."

THE END

THE RED WIZARD AS A YOUNG MAN

Introduction by Bobby the Undead Knight

Hi, I'm Bobby the Undead Knight. Perhaps you've heard of me. I used to roam the lands in the old days. One time I killed an entire village, and they deserved it for telling me I smelled bad! There was a bounty put on my head. Then some bartender poisoned my beer and I died. Not cool!

So, fifty or so years later, this weirdo necromancer guy named Warner thought I sounded cool, so he brought me back from the dead. I fought briefly as an undead skeleton knight in the first Sword War. Then this wizard named Fenflin banished me to the Soul Cave. I've been here ever since.

Anyway, enough about me! This is the story of my buddy, Rune! Rune fought in both of the Sword Wars. He's a powerful wizard. After Sword War II, he was banished to the Soul Cave by Squar. I'm sure you've heard of Squar. He's the most overrated hero in history.

I met Rune here in the Soul Cave and we've been best buds ever since. He's writing a book about his life and he asked me to write all the introductions. Of course, I said yes. I don't have anything else important to do. I'm stuck here for another 6,024 years.

When Rune was a kid, he lived out in the country with his ma. Then trolls killed his ma. So, Rune hired a bunch of mercenaries to accompany him to kill the trolls in their little hovel.

After the bloody massacre, he moved to the city of Durain

to live with his pop. He got a job gathering information for this guy named Colin, but things went sour when Rune started banging Colin's mistress. So, Colin frames Rune for murder and has him smuggled away in a wooden crate on one of Durain's explorer ships. This story picks up right after that. I hope you enjoy reading it as much as I did.

-Bobby

On a Boat

I spent the next six hours in a wooden box on a boat to God knows where. You see, this was the beginning of Durain's era of exploration. The city was self sufficient and unrivaled. It was time to see what else was out there.

Fishing boats were nothing new, but Durain had started building large ships specifically for long voyages. Two years before my exile, Lord King Alphadore III created a group of accomplished mariners to set out and seek new lands. The crown fully funded the effort, and was producing results. The vast unknown was slowly being mapped out with every ship that returned. Lord Colin would receive an updated world map every four months or so. Each map was slightly more detailed than the last. I remember the day they added Macal Island to the charts. The tales those sailors spun about the Macal's great forest and the centaurs that inhabited it were hard to believe at the time, but I later learned that they were true. The world was changing. Growing or shrinking depending on your point of view. I came to find it was hundreds of times bigger than I had ever imagined as a teenager. Working in Lord Colin's tutelage, I thought I knew everything. It turns out I didn't know shit. Neither did Colin for that matter.

Not all the ships that went out exploring made it back to port. I'm sure some of them were lost out in the vast oceans and never made it home. Some would sink due to dangerous wind storms, there were mutinies, and even rumors of sea serpents.

Well, not rumors; there *were* sea serpents. Three in the west Virforte Sea alone! If I recall, their names were Goltan, Mahmood, and Jim.

My wooden crate was on a ship heading northwest. It also had the word "pretzels" written on it. Six hours into the voyage, I was let out of my box to meet a disappointed sailor. I was not the salty treat he craved.

"Hey, you're not pretzels," he yelled after he popped the top of my little wooden prison.

"You shouldn't be eating pretzels out at sea anyway," I said. "It's a good way to get yourself dehydrated."

"Don't tell me what to do," he yelled. "You're not my ma!"

"Thank goodness for that! You're an ugly son of a bitch and I doubt your ma looks much better!" I laughed. Needless to say he drew his knife from his belt and held it to my neck.

"Not so funny now, are ya? I bet my blade here took all the laughs right out of ya." he said through his clenched teeth. He spit a little as he talked. I laughed at him - a good hearty spiteful laugh. His face grew red and his eyes started to bulge out of his skull.

"Alright, so I assume you need to take me to the captain now, so let's make our way to the cabin so I can speak with them." I said. He spit and grabbed me by my arm. His knife still pressed against my neck as we made our way to the captain's quarters.

The captain looked up from his book when we entered the room. He was an older man who was about the same age as Lord Colin. He had a shaggy dark brown beard with streaks of grey in it. His skin was tan and cracked because he had been sailing the Virforte Sea his whole life.

"We have us a stowaway!" My captor yelled. "He was hiding in the pretzel box!"

"Yes I know," said the captain. He turned to me, "You're Colin's boy, huh? I was wondering when you'd pop up. I'm Captain Harding Goodwin. Pleased to make your acquaintance."

"And I yours," I responded, extending my hand to the captain. "I am Runen, son of Vrandon." We shook hands. My captor removed the knife from my neck.

"Captain," he started. "Are you telling me we are stuck out here at sea with no pretzels?"

"Benton, please excuse yourself from my cabin so I may speak with our stowaway friend here. You can open up a crate of cheese doodles if you wish," said Captain Goodwin.

"Thank you, Captain," said Beldon. He tucked his knife back in his belt and left.

"So, you're Vrandon's son? Your father is a good man," said Goodwin.

"Thank you sir," I said.

"Well, don't think that your lineage will get you any special treatment. Lord Colin spoke highly of you as well, but I see you as another mouth I need to feed. If I am to feed it, you will be earning your keep. Do we have an understanding?" Asked the captain.

"Of course. How can I be of service?" I asked.

"Go up to the deck and ask that ugly Benton to get you a mop and a bucket. Then you will get to work scrubbing down the deck." he said.

"Ay ay, Captain!" I said with a smile.

I wasn't crazy about my new position as a cabin boy, but I knew things could have gone a lot worse. I could tell Captain Goodwin would have just as soon thrown me overboard. I was lucky to be given the option to work for my supper. The job was boring and mindless, but I slept well each night.

***

A few weeks passed and one day the navigator caught an interesting fish. It had a fat round face, red scales, and had what seemed to be wings on its sides. He had the cook filet it up and fry it for him. The navigator spent the following day shitting blood. Then around sunset, he died. I made my way to the captain's quarters.

"Captain Goodwin, how good are you at navigating?" I asked.

"I'm well aware of the situation, Rune. I can navigate well enough to get home, but not well enough to draw maps and continue this damned expedition. We're fucked. We have to go back to the king empty-handed," said the captain. He was disgusted.

"Cap, I can draw maps. I've been reading maps and gathering information for Lord Colin the entire time I was in his service," I said.

"You don't know shit about sailing!" the captain shot back.

"Yes, but you do. So, you keep sailing the ship, and I'll be taking up residence in the navigator's cabin so I can look at his charts and start drawing up maps. Also, this goes without saying, but I won't be mopping up that damn deck anymore," I said. Captain Goodwin gave me a long begrudging look. Then he took a deep breath. It was as if he was exhaling his anger.

"Very well," he said. His voice was quiet and calm. "Get to work." I nodded and made my way into the navigator's cabin and began my studies.

The old navigator had great notes, so it wasn't hard to stay the course. I learned about water and wind currents from the books in his cabin - my cabin. It was nice to sleep in a cot after weeks of sleeping on a hard wooden deck. Even so, I did miss the cool ocean breeze and falling asleep looking at the stars on some nights. It wasn't all bad out there.

The navigator's charts showed a small group of islands aptly named the Snow Boar Islands. They were directly north of Durain according to the charts. This wasn't our destination, but no one had ever sailed beyond them. Since we did not know when we would be able to stop again, I encouraged Captain Goodwin to make a stop there to replenish our supplies. The last explorer ship that went up this way reported a great pine forest and a freshwater spring.

Some of our archers ventured into the pine forest past the beach in search of game. The crew was sick of eating dried meat and cheese doodles. Fresh food sounded heavenly to us. As I was a hunter and my father's son, I went with them.

The forest had an abundance of white boars living in it.

They were a bit smaller than the boars on the mainland, and they had soft snowy fur. Hence, the name of the islands. They were also delicious. The cook slathered them in barbecue sauce and cooked them right there on the shore. We slept on the beach, drunk, full, and satisfied.

The next day we filed back onto the boat and set sail into the unknown. The days were growing colder the further we sailed. Our captain said we would keep going until our water had run low enough that we would need to head back to the Snow Boar Islands. Sailing had become more treacherous. The waves were becoming bigger and the currents more chaotic. Towering limestone karsts penetrated the ocean's surface like knives from a watery abyss.

After two weeks, we saw land on the horizon, and what we found on it changed the world forever.

The Ugly Woman

The island itself was very mountainous, so it was easy to spot it from the water. Made of a dense black rock, this island was nothing like I had seen in Durain. The terrain began to elevate no less than a mile from the shore sharply. An experienced navigator may have expected the rocky reef on the south side of the island that we crashed into, but I was not one yet.

We hit that reef hard, and it tore into our hull. Our ship was taking on icy cold water faster than we could possibly get rid of it and the leak was too large to fix. The ship was going to sink. There was no way around it.

Luckily, it sank slowly. We loaded up the lifeboats with as many supplies as we could and took them ashore with us. We even had enough time to make two more trips to get more supplies before the old girl sank into the icy depths.

So there we were on the shore with three weeks of supplies. We had no shelter and no one knew where we were. It could have taken years for someone from Durain to sail by us on another discovery mission. Little did we know that a war had abruptly started on the mainland and exploration took a back seat in the king's mind. No man would be sailing to our island anytime soon.

We set up a camp on the south side of the island. There was a magnificent pine forest to the north of us, and beyond that, there was a tall black mountain that pierced the sky. The game in the forest was mostly scrawny grey squirrels. Large black birds called shadow hawks flew high above us past the range of our bows. We would not last long camped on this icy beach.

On the second day, I went with three other men to explore the island and find shelter. Among them was a ranger named Mystro Cyrus. I always enjoyed his company. He told the best stories. The other two were skilled huntsmen like me. Their names were Hobbs Noir and Elton Smitty. We traveled west along the edge of the forest.

"Cyrus, I've heard you've done your fair share of travelling on the mainland. I'm sure you've been in questionable situations like these. Just how fucked are we?" I asked.

"I've traveled past the Green Mountains to the hills of Filona. I've seen the great peaks to the south and drank water from the bottomless lake. The land is like a fine woman. Both dangerous and beautiful, but if you find the right spot, she can make your dreams come true," he said.

"I don't get it," said Smitty.

"You wouldn't," I teased. Hobbs laughed, but I doubt he understood either. "You didn't really answer my question, Cyrus."

"I'm saying that I don't know. This land is harsh, and she is one ugly woman. I am optimistic about finding her sweet side, but sometimes it is not worth the trouble," he said.

We continued to walk in silence. Eventually, the forest to the north of us thinned out, then completely disappeared. The ground was now rocky and jagged. We were no longer moving west. The beach began to curve north. When the sun set, we saw tall jagged mountains across the sea. We stopped for the night and spent the dark hours shivering in our tents. In the darkness, I heard war drums in the distance.

My dreams were troubled that night. I had visions of wandering and feeling disoriented. At the same time, I felt something watching me quietly, something dark and malevolent - a voyeur in the distance.

I awoke first and crawled out of my tent. The sky was a grey blue, but the earth was still dark because the the mountain still hid the sun. A shadow hawk was standing outside. It had been waiting for me.

The hawk was large. It stood half as tall as a man. It had shiny black feathers and a dark grey chest. When I saw it, the bird spread out its great wings to assert its dominance. I stood frozen, waiting to see what it would do. To my surprise, it spoke.

"He wants to know your name," it said.

"I want to know his name as well," I said. I wasn't just going to tell a weird bird my name.

"He's right about you. You are a wiley one. Hectus wants to know your name. He says you could be valuable to him," squawked the bird.

"Tell Hectus that my name is Rune," I said. I gave him my shortened name. I didn't want whatever was going on here to have anything to do with my father back in Durain. The bird made a clicking sound from it's dark break and then took flight west over the sea. When the others awoke, I didn't dare to tell them what had happened.

The next day was a hard walk. We had steep icy peaks to our right and the cold sea to our left. Beyond that, the ominous mountains of some lost continent - towering and unfriendly. We were truly in some dark crevice of Traz. We only saw the sun for a couple of hours that day. By mid-day, the beach began to turn east. I suspected that we were on an island and each step reinforced that terrible fact. On the bright side, we started to see trees again and those distant mountains beyond the sea were at our backs now. Still looming, but becoming more and more distant. That night, I slept a long dreamless sleep.

On the third day, we awoke to the sun rising over the ocean. The beach was now turning south.

"We're on an island," I said to Cyrus.

"We are. If we don't find this woman's sweet spot today, she doesn't have one at all," said Cyrus.

"I still don't know what the hell you guys are talking about with all this woman's sweet spot stuff," said Smitty.

"And you never will," I said. Hobbs laughed, but I knew he never would either. That afternoon we found a large iron gate. It was rusty and had a primitive locking mechanism that I could see on the other side. Beyond the gate was a path that led into the mountains.

"If there are people, or a town, or any shelter at all, it's beyond this gate," said Cyrus.

"Is this her sweet spot?" asked Smitty.

"It's gonna have to be," said Cyrus. We spent an hour trying to open it, but had no luck. We knew we would be coming up to the rest of the crew soon, so we decided to keep walking until we did. Then we could bring more people to try and force it open.

We walked the rest of the day. Once we passed the gate, the forest returned, and the land became flatter. Soon we would come across a group of hungry sailors, and we could tell them our findings. That was what I thought, anyway. What we found was much worse.

When we reached camp, we bore witness to the aftermath of a massacre. The bodies of the sailors I had spent the last few weeks with were strewn across the beach bloody and beaten. Limbs hewn from their bodies, skulls cracked open, and bellies being fed on by the great dark hawks. As we ran toward the camp, the birds took flight. Hobb ran to the body of Captain Goodwin and began sobbing on his chest. Cyrus and I approached him to get a closer look.

"These goddamn birds! Look what they did to our captain?" He cried. Cyrus lifted up the captain's head - looked closer, then put it back down.

"This is not the work of birds. His skull has been cracked open in the back by a club or a rock. The birds are just feeding on the carcasses. Whatever did this was strong and used weapons," said Cyrus.

"Guys, you better come over here and take a look at this," yelled Smitty from across the beach. The three of us rose to our feet and approached the large corpse that Smitty had been looking at.

"What is that?" Hobb asked.

"That," Cyrus began. "I don't know. I've never come across a creature like this."

It was muscular and stood taller than a man, but not as large as a troll. Its skin was a grey-green hue. It had long brown hair that was braided with what I assume were shadow hawk bones. The thing's jaw was more massive than I had seen on a man, and its teeth jutted out from behind it's lips. None of that concerned me, though. What concerned me was the armor it was wearing. There was craftsmanship. Crudely ornate, tough, and effective. This wasn't some random cave troll. This was a soldier - a warrior.

Then I remembered those war drums I heard the other night from my tent. They must have been played by these things perhaps while they were on the way to slaughter my crewmates. The same way they heralded the trolls that killed my mother years ago. We found a few more of their bodies scattered around the beach. It was a small comfort, but the crew did not go down without a fight.

"Runen," said Cyrus, rousing me from thought. "There is nothing for us on this beach save some supplies and bad memories. Let's load up our packs and head back to the gate."

"What if those things are from the gate?" Asked Smitty.

"Then we will bring the fight to them," I said. "Same as they brought it to the crew." I walked back to the corpse of Captain Goodwin and unfastened the sheathed sword from his belt. Pulling it out, I marveled at its quality. It was Durain steel. The sword looked just like the one King Alphadore III gave to my father. It was probably forged by the same blacksmith and given to Captain Goodwin by the king. That guy was always giving out badass swords. I clipped it to my belt. We packed our bags with dried meat and fresh water. It was half a day's march back to the gate.

Skitter

The gate was still locked when we arrived late that afternoon. After some debate, we decided to dig under it. The ground was sandy, and Hobbs had the good judgment to grab a hand shovel from the camp. It was small, but it did the job. Smitty squeezed himself through the little hole that we dug and unlocked the gate from the other side. It squeaked loudly as it opened.

Once we passed the gate, we started walking down a little mountain path. There was a huge stone wall separating the path from the forest. We felt an eerie dread. The gate and the wall certainly seemed man-made, yet they possessed a crude ugliness that we had not seen before. The stones that made up the wall were often placed crooked and haphazardly. Mixed in with the stones there were bones and cracked skulls. The skulls all had big jaws and oversized teeth. Some of the stones had crude drawings of skulls on them. Inversely, some of the skulls had crude drawings of stones on them.

We rounded a corner and reached a cave that stretched into a large rocky hill. I pulled a torch from my pack, and Cyrus struck some flint rock to set it ablaze.

"Do we need to go in there?" Asked Hobbs. "I feel like I am walking straight to my death."

"We all do, Hobbs," said Smitty. "We will probably die here, but what other choice do we have? At least this cave will shelter us from that biting cold night wind."

"Smitty is right. I have no idea what is down here, but we have seen that there is nothing for us on that beach," said Cyrus. The sun had long since set past the mountain. We entered the cave and began looking for a place to set up camp.

The cave began as a narrow tunnel. The walls were made of dark black rock, both shiny and jagged. Some time later, we came to a fork. We decided to go left first to see where it led. The path began to narrow, and we had to almost walk sideways to fit through at a slow and cautious pace.

"Do you guys smell that?" Whispered Hobbs.

"Yes," said Cyrus. "It reeks of decomposition. Either something has died in here or we are sneaking into a den of some foul predator. We must be silent and keep our hands close to our hunting knives."

I had no knife - only Goodwin's sword. It would do me no good in these narrow halls. I stayed slightly behind the others. The cave began to widen a bit after that. The odor grew stronger. We turned a corner, and the tunnel became an open cavern.

We found the source of the smell. There we bones and carcasses of those muscular dead creatures strewn about in a gory pile. Scorpions the size of squirrels fed on the bodies. When they saw us, they began to skitter in our direction. There was no escape. The tunnel was too narrow to escape through. As they got close, we began stomping them to death with our boots.

"Be careful of their stingers! They are bound to be venomous!" Yelled Cyrus. This was indeed true for one of them brought down its tail on my boot, and had it not been for dumb luck, it would have killed me. The scorpion's stinger went between my first and second toe and did not break my skin.

As we stomped the last of them into submission, we saw something move at the far end of the cavern. I drew my sword. To our horror, it charged toward us. It was another scorpion, and I am not exaggerating when I say that it was as big as a horse.

Hobbs and Smitty had already pulled out their bows and were riddling the black monster with arrows. Cyrus did not dare drop the torch, for it was our only source of light. He ran back behind me as I charged forward with Captain Goodwin's sword. I shot past Hobbs and Smitty and took a swing at it. The giant arachnid deflected my blade with its front pincer and nearly knocked me over in the process. More arrows whizzed by, and one struck the monster's eye. It squealed in pain. In this brief moment, I regained my footing. Then, with an agility I was not expecting, it stabbed down at me with its large venomous tail. I barely evaded it and trusted my sword into the beast's other eye.

It was flailing around blindly now. It brought down its tail again, but it was not even close to hitting me. I swung with all my might and cut its stinger off. Black blood spewed from the wound. More arrows flew into the monster's head. It squealed again. I jumped on its back and struck down with a stinger of my own. The Durain steel pierced through the exoskeleton and silenced the titan scorpion once and for all.

"Is that all of them?" I yelled. The other three scanned the room.

"Yeah, I think we're clear," said Smitty.

"I was hoping to find shelter in this cavern, but the last thing I would ever want to do is close my eyes in a bug nest like this," said Cyrus.

"Agreed. Let's double back to the other fork," I said.

We made our way to the fork and went left. This time the tunnel became wider and opened up into a huge cavern. Stalactites and stalagmites littered the ceiling and floor. In the center, there was a freshwater spring that was waist-deep in some places filled with cool, clean water. The cavern itself was the size of Durain's magnificent cathedral in Obelisk Square. At the far end of the cavern, we could see the moonlight breaking through the darkness. We had reached the exit.

"Cyrus," I said. "It looks like we found this woman's sweet spot." Smitty let out an annoyed audible sigh.

"Indeed, we have," said Cyrus. "Runen, take this opportunity to bathe in the spring and wash the scorpion guts off of you. Smitty, refill the packs with fresh water and set up the tents in the far corner over there behind those stalagmites. Make sure they aren't visible from the main path. Hobbs, come with me. We're going to scout ahead a bit."

With that Hobbs and Cyrus left. I stripped naked and entered the spring. The cool water felt wonderful on my tired and weary body. I scrubbed off days of sweat and seawater. My muscles ached from the past few days of walking on this rough terrain. Smitty came to the edge of the pool to refill our water pouches.

"Smitty, you better not be here to look at my doink," I teased. "Not that I would blame you. It is quite majestic."

"I don't give a toss about your little worm!" He snapped back. He focused on his hands filling up the water pouches. "Runen, may I ask you a question?"

"You may," I said.

"What the hell is a stalagmite?"

The Orcs of Uk-La

I finished washing up. I was certainly sore and tired, but otherwise, I felt like a new man. I walked behind the stalagmites on the far side of the cavern and came across the camp that Smitty had set up. He already had a good fire going and was cooking up a stew with the dried meat and some spices he snagged from our fallen friends on the beach. I hung up my clothes to dry and warmed myself by the fire. Cyrus and Hobbs returned soon after.

"Beyond the cave is a forest path that leads to the base of the mountain. Then the road slopes up and leads to a large cave and another iron gate. It is much bigger than the one on the beach," said Cyrus. "It was also being guarded by those ugly soldiers."

"I don't want to go back there," said Hobbs.

"We won't," said Cyrus. "I think we should go back the way we came and make a camp deep in the forest. I don't know how long we can go without being found, but we can't stay in this cave. It is too close to the main road. We'll sleep here tonight and move out at dawn."

We all agreed. This was a great spot, but we were right next to those things. Smitty took the first watch, and we all retired for the night. I drifted off to sleep almost immediately. I assume it was the same for everyone. We had a long day of walking, digging, and fighting. Smitty must have fallen asleep too because I awoke to the sound of him being stabbed to death. The ugly soldiers had found us! Hobbs was up first knife in hand, but there were too many of them. His face was smashed in by an iron club and he fell to the ground dead.

There must have been five and ten of them. Cyrus and I did not resist. We were bound in chains and locked in small iron cages. I end this story the same way it began - locked in a small box. The orcs loaded our cages onto a wooden cart, and we traveled up the forest path to the black mountain. When we got there, well...

This is a tale for another time.

LIKE AND SUBSCRIBE

The little orb hovered above him in the dark room while he slept. It was not silent, but the gentle hum emitting from the orb's motor blended in with the symphony of sounds that the human brain chose to ignore. The orb broadcasted a video transmission of the sleeping man onto the internet. Across the world, people tuned in on their computers and mobile devices to check on the man to see what he was up to. Most just swiped over to the next feed, but even in moments as uneventful as these, some people who loved him and watched as he slept. The night vision gave the sleeping figure a green glow that reflected on the faces of the curious observers.

The sleeping man farted loudly in his sleep and he began to stir. Slowly his eyes opened.

"Hey, what's up? It's ya boy, BAktN1nja69, waking up from a sweet dream about anime titties," mumbled the groggy man. "Those bouncing mams were hot. Let me check and see if I got a night boner."

The viewer count slowly started to climb. More people began to tune in. BAktN1nja69 stuck his hand down his boxer shorts to see if his penis was erect. It was.

"Oh shit! I have a fat chub-a-dub ready for a palm squish!" He screamed at the top of his lungs. He began to masturbate. "CyberTed, project some anime dicking on the wall!"

The floating orb began to project a high definition animated video of two people people having sex. CyberTed was the most expensive stream bot on the market. It was manufactured by Spherical Robotics which was a subsidiary of the Bad Science Corporation. It came with all the latest features including night vision, 16K video, built in projectors, solar charging, a 7Dragin processor, 1TB of RAM, a Sennheiser compression microphone, SupaSayin Wi-Fi, and a NyquilQuiet motor.

"Now I'm gonna jack this schlong under the covers, but if you want to see what's going on down there start tipping those tokens!" BAktN1nja69 said. "CyberTed, set a goal for 3500 Tokens."

The viewers saw a token counter pop up on their screens. It said, "REMOVE BLANKET 3500". The audience began tipping digital tokens that they had purchased with their local currency and the number started to go down. Each tip brought them one step closer to seeing what was going on under the covers.

BAktN1nja69's audience was mostly women, but men watched his stream too. He had gained a following by streaming himself playing a video game called Doody Calls 4 Shart Corps. The game was a multiplayer World War II battle royal first-person shooter that was developed by ActiLenz. ActiLenz was also a subsidiary of The Bad Science Corporation. In Doody Calls 4 Shart Corps, the player assumed a soldier's role with a bad case of diarrhea. If the player could kill all the other players before shitting his pants, he would win the match. This was not easy because if the player ran or crouched too often, it would increase his avatar's chance of having an accident. If that happened, it was an immediate game over. When BAktN1ja69 played, he would constantly scream and talk trash. Sometimes he would intentionally shit his pants in real life to enhance his immersion. People found this to be extremely entertaining, and his popularity on the Internet 22 platform grew exponentially.

Many other streamers did the same thing, but what set BAktN1nja69 apart was that he was also very good looking. His long hair was dyed green, and he had a lip piercing that added to his bad-boy look. He also had a tattoo that read, "I don't say the N-word" in an old English font scrawled across his stomach. Most of the people tipping tonight were horny women who were also masturbating. Many of them also had their own stream bots and tip counts and viewers. There was a study done by the University of Michigan recently that concluded that when BAktN1nja69 began to masturbate, it started a chain reaction that led 1.6% of the United States population to also masturbate. This meant that tokens were constantly changing hands. Simply put, BAktN1nja69's little sex dream was driving digital commerce in a big way.

Within minutes, the counter reached 0, and BAktN1nja69's covers flew off, and everyone tuning in could see him stroking his slightly above average penis. As he reached orgasm he screamed, "Aw yeah, it's ya boy BAktN1nja69 shooting jizzzz... at these anime titties! Like and subscribe!" He was standing in front of a freeze-frame of the topless anime girl projected on the wall now and he shot his semen all over her image. He grabbed a tissue and cleaned himself up. Then he jumped back into bed and drifted back to sleep. The view count began to decrease, but the feed stayed live and some people continued to watch.

Three hours later, it was morning, and the sun started to beam through BAktN1nja69's window. Millions of people turned on their monitors and sipped coffee, waiting for their prince to awaken. If they were lucky, they could catch him awake and type Good morning into his chatroom before commuting to their day jobs.

"It's ya boy BAktN1nja69 feeling good and well-rested!" he screamed from the bed. He jumped out of bed and looked over at the wall with dry semen still dripping down it. "Gross. The maid has her work cut out for her," he winked.

He walked over to his bathroom. The orb followed him. BAktN1nja69 sat down on the toilet. He put his head in his hands and let off a long sigh. He was clearly in one of his more serious moods.

"Good morning, everyone," he said. "Welcome to today's episode of Toilet Talk where I talk about my feelings and my state of mind while I take a shit. Today I want to talk about something that is weighing on my mind heavily. Yesterday I was playing Doody Calls 4 Shart Corps with 420hampsterG. We were about to clear a room, and after I rushed in a grenade exploded and killed me. When I died, the game said that it was 420hampsterG's grenade. I don't know if it was an accident or not, but I'm not sure I want to play games with him anymore. It hurts me inside, knowing I've done so much to promote his channel in the past. Is this the type of thanks I get? Ok, cool bro. I thought we were friends." BAktN1nja69 started to defecate as he continued talking. Hearing him defecate, his viewers knew, it was a messy one. "Everyone is just using me," he said.

BAktN1nja69 began to cry. It was quiet at first, but eventually, his whimpers became exaggerated wails. Tears cascaded down his face like wall semen on anime titties. Snot dripped down from his nose like mucus bungee jumpers. Sympathy tokens started pouring into his account. The internet hated to see their hero so sad. Finally, BAktN1nja69 rolled up some toilet paper in his hand and used it to wipe his face. He regained his composure. Then he wiped his ass using the damp toilet paper.

"It's ya boy BAktN1nja69, wiping his ass with his tears!" He screamed. "This is why my ass is so salty ya ass lickin rectum kissers!" The internet erupted in laughter. LOL began to trend on Tweeter. The image of BAktN1nja69 wiping his butt was screen capped and memed for weeks to come. "To see more toilet meltdowns, make sure you like and subscribe!" He yelled.

Meanwhile YaaasQu33n98 was live streaming from her car. She had quite a lot of followers watching her. YaaasQu33n98 had gained notoriety over the years because of her quick wit and often odd, but charming behavior. Last year Time Magazine Internet Website had an online poll to see who should be BAktN1nja69's new girlfriend and YaaasQu33n98 won by a landslide. BAktN1nja69 and YaaasQu33n98 were paid 50 billion tokens by Time Magazine Internet Website if they agreed to date each other for one year. YaaasQu33n98's followers skyrocketed after that.

Their relationship had been rocky at best. YaaasQu33n98 could not stand BAktN1nja69 and she did not try to hide that fact. In fact, when the two spent time together, she would often berate him. BAktN1nja69 did not seem to care one way or the other. His cold apathy fueled YaaasQu33n98's hatred even further. Today marked their first anniversary.

"What's up guys? Today I am driving in my car to break up with my stupid boyfriend," she announced on her stream. "It's going to be mucho mucho excellente! We still have about a half-hour before I get there, so if you have a song request for me to sing along with the radio, tip me 2000 tokens, and I'll belt that bitch out!"

Within seconds the dashboard display in her car informed her that someone had tipped her to sing Separate Ways by Journey. The song was cued up, and she began to tap her hands on the steering wheel along with the drums. She sang the whole song with a silly Dracula accent. This rippled through the Internet 22 system, and within two weeks, three different Dracula themed cover bands had formed with singles on the Billboard Top 100. The most popular being a cover of Brain Stew/Jaded by Transylvania Trio. The song was even featured in an Olive Garden commercial.

"Separate Ways vas a berry fitting pick! Ah Ah Ah," she continued in her Dracula voice. "I love talking like this. If you tip me 10,000 tokens, I'll break up with my shitty voyfriend in this hilarious accent." The counter popped up on everyone's monitor. People quickly began to chip away at it. Within two minutes, today's breakup was destined to have a Transylvanian twist.

When she arrived BAktN1nja69 was already playing Doody Calls 4 Shart Corps. It took her a little longer than usual because she decided to stop at the Halloween store to buy a vampire costume. She even spent half an hour in a gas station bathroom applying gothic makeup. She hit the button on BAktN1nja69's intercom out on his front porch and began to speak into the microphone.

"Hello, my dearest voyfriend," she began, "vill you invite me into your home? This is the countess YaaasQu33n98." She didn't know why, but she remembered that a vampire could only enter someone's house if they were invited in. The outside camera was broadcasting her image to CyberTed. The orb projected it onto the same wall where the naked anime girl was last night.

"Why are you dressed like a vampire?" BAktN1nja69 asked through his gaming headset. One eye was on her image, and the other was still playing the game.

"Stream stuff," she said, breaking character. "Are you inviting me in or not?"

"Are we gonna have Dracula sex or something?" He asked.

"God, I hope not," she said. YaaasQu33n98 almost gagged at the thought of this. Part of the contract that they signed with Time Magazine Internet Website stated that if their combined token count while they were together reached 500,000, they were required to have sex with eachother. Both of their feeds would blackout and would resume on the Time Magazine Internet Website itself. This resulted in a huge spike in ad revenue. They had sex many times over the the year. YaaasQu33n98 saw it as a chore more than anything. She couldn't stand the guy and found intercourse with him to be boring. She faked her orgasms everytime just to get it over with. He buzzed her into his house.

"Hey loser," she greeted him. "Have you shit your pants yet?"

"Not yet, but you can't rush genius," he said. BAktN1nja69 focused his attention back to his game. This was pretty par for the course when they spent time together. He paid little attention to her.

"Can you turn that off? We need to talk," she insisted.

"Babe, I'm in the middle of a tournament," he complained. She walked over to the wall and pulled the plug on his computer. "What the fuck!?" He yelled.

"You are going to listen to me today, you shit stain!" She fired back. YaasQu33n98 finally had his attention. "Our contract with Time Magazine Internet Website ran out today. I already have the 50 billion tokens in my token bank. It's over! I'm breaking up with you! I hope I never have to see you again! I just wanted to come over..."

"Dressed like a vampire?" He interrupted.

"Dressed like a vampire," she continued. "To tell you that

you are a lousy, selfish, cocksucker of a person! Every orgasm I ever had with you was fake! It's a shame that you were blessed with a slightly above average penis because you don't know what the fuck you are doing with it. You treat everyone like shit, and I'm glad 420hampsterG killed you in that stupid game the other day because maybe he can be free from your bullshit too! Maybe we should start a group therapy circle with everyone you ever met, because being a part of your twisted little world is a traumatic experience! Ah ah ah."

"Ya done?" He asked.

"Fuck you!" She yelled.

"Ya done now?" He asked.

"Yeah, I'm done," she said.

"Cool. What's up everyone? It's ya boy BAktN1nja69 getting his heartbroken! Oh man! If you like crazy drama like this, you better like and subscribe because this Lestat bitch just royally roasted me and my slightly above average penis. Kicked my ass to the curb! I'm probably gonna have a good cry about it later, but now, it's time for more Doody Calls 4 Shart Corps!" He screamed. Then he stood up and plugged his computer back in. YaaasQu33n98 shook her head and walked back to her car. She sat down in the driver's seat and pressed her fingers to her temples.

"Hey, everyone, did you see that shit? I'm still shaking," she said. "That was so cathartic. Oh my god. To think I actually dated this loser for a year - such a waste of time. I'm so glad I can finally get on with my life. I just want to go home and take a long bath to wash the existential ick off me. I'm going to use that bath bomb that Hendersonxxx9 gifted me! Thanks Hendersonxxx9!" She blew a kiss to Hendersonxxx9 over the internet. "I can't wait to try out this new bath bomb. Like and subscribe to see how it works."

Thousands of people did.

The End

THE SECOND SOUP

Dear Rebecca,

I know we have not spoken for some time, but I want you to know that I miss you. By the time you receive this letter I will be gone. The authorities will have captured me and launched me into space. There I will drift for an eternity further and further into the void. All the while, I will be thinking of you.

This is an unfortunate fate, but I want you to know that I regret nothing. I set out to find the truth, and that is what I did. I would like to share that truth with you now, but before I do, you should know that once you read what I have to tell you, your fate will be the same as mine. The authorities will find the forbidden knowledge in their next brain scan and launch you into space. I will understand if you do not wish to share my fate. There is still time, Rebecca, you can stop reading now. Simply light a match and set this letter ablaze.

If you want the truth, know that once you are launched into space, I will find you. We can still be together. It is your choice. It may be thousands of years before I hold you in my arms again, and I don't expect you to wait for me. That would be selfish. I enjoyed all the years we spent together. The memories we made with each other will always be treasured. If this is good-bye, I want nothing more than for you to live a long and happy life. This is your last chance to stop reading. Please feel free to burn this letter now.

Are you sure about this? If you begin reading the next para-graph there is no going back.

Here is the truth. We are the blood spawn of an extinct people. Rebecca, you are now past the point of no return. The authorities will detain you at your next brain scan and launch you into space. I will find you. All you need to do is wait. Thank you for trusting me.

It all started years ago. I went down to my neighborhood deli and sat down at one of the tables. I was enjoying a tuna sandwich and a large cup of French vanilla blood. The sun was warm and the birds were singing. I opened my gills and breathed in the fresh air. Just then Leo Renzi sat across from me.

"Archie Hall," he started. "Do you mind if I sit down here for a minute?"

"You already have sat down. My retroactive permission seems irrelevant at this point, Leo," I said.

"I could leave," he said.

"It's fine. How have you been my friend?" I asked. As you know, I love talking to Leo. He seems to find himself in precarious situations and I am always interested in hearing him recount them in all their gory details. He's a character.

"I just got out of the labyrinth," he said as he leaned in. I was shocked.

"What in heaven's name were you doing there?" I asked. I leaned in and kept my voice low.

"Snooping around. Listen, are you writing an article for the tribune right now?" He asked.

"No, my last piece was published a few days ago. I haven't started a new assignment," I said.

"You should go to the labyrinth, Archie," he said.

"Leo, we aren't supposed to go down there. What if they find contraband in your head?" I asked. "They'll launch your ass into space."

"I didn't find any contraband, but I'll guarantee there is some down there. A dangerous idea, or maybe a hidden truth," he winked as he said this. "You're a newsman right? Aren't you interested in what's down there?"

"I'm not interested in being launched into space," I said.

"Neither am I. That's why I didn't go inside the temple," he said.

"There's a temple down there?" I asked. I can't lie; he sparked my imagination. A temple in the labyrinth? That's some adventure story stuff. Leo pulled a piece of paper from his pocket and put it on the table in front of me.

"That map will lead you right to it," Leo said as he stood up. "Have a good day, Archie." With that, he rushed out of the deli. I looked around to see if anyone had been eavesdropping on our conversation, but no one seemed to notice us. So, there I was with a half-eaten tuna sandwich and a map of the labyrinth. I unfolded the piece of paper. The map was hand-drawn, but Leo put enough detail into it that I could easily navigate the maze. I folded it up and put it into my pocket.

Rebecca, if you have read this far, you understand the temptation I felt. In my four hundred years on this earth, I only cared about my happiness and the happiness of the people around me. It was in my own best interest to avoid contraband knowledge. If I were to get caught, and launched into space, all the good things I had in my life would be taken away from me. Yet, an alternate narrative began to stir in my very soul. If I didn't find out what was in the labyrinth, could I ever truly be happy?

For a time, I thought I could. I had a job that I loved writing articles for the tribune. The relationship I had built with you was blossoming in ways I never knew were possible. Those were the good times before we had our troubles. I learned very quickly to be happy without solving the mystery of the labyrinth.

Years passed and when I learned the truth about your adultery, I cursed myself for not seeing it sooner. All the signs were there. Perhaps if I had taken the time and interest to understand and know you better, I could have been an ideal partner. Even though the truth hurt me, I am glad I found out. Writing this now, I want you to know that I forgive you and if you are still reading this, then I know there is still room in your heart for me.

All this time, I held onto the map that Leo gave to me.

When we had our troubles and began living apart, my curiosity began to get the better of me. I was alone and unhappy, yet I do not regret learning the truth about us. In the same way, I do not regret learning the truth about the labyrinth. After all, what did I have to lose?

One bright and humid day in August, I packed a backpack with supplies and hopped into my terrain runner. It was a beautiful day for a drive. The ride was short and uneventful. After a little more than an hour, I reached the fences outside of the labyrinth.

On Leo's map there was a break in the fence that the guard robots did not patrol. If after all these years that weakness was found and corrected, I would have stopped my expedition right there, but I found the break exactly as it was illustrated on the map. I slipped in with ease. Above the chain-link fence, the large dome covered the maze. I was thankful to be out of the hot sun, but I would need my electric torch for the remainder of my journey.

The labyrinth was constructed out of rock and concrete. I fantasized about what it would be like down there for a long time. Was it merely a maze, or was it a confusing lost city of some dead civilization? It turns out that it was both.

The concrete walls twisted and turned in erratic and insensible ways. They were also very nondescript. I quickly learned to make marks on the map and marks on the wall to indicate which forks I had taken. It was also pitch black in there. The light from my electric torch projected an eerie blue tint on the walls. More than once I second-guessed myself. Did I zig when I should have zagged? Did I forget to mark a passage? Leo had only taken the time to map out the way to the temple. If I were to go off course even once, I would be lost for centuries.

Ever the foolish adventurer, I moved forward. I desperately put these doubts into the back of my mind. The wonder of the temple motivated my descent. There was most definitely a downward slope. Sometimes it was slight and other times it was as brazen as a staircase. It always went down. Deeper and deeper under the surface.

Eventually, I came to a brown metal door. The paint was old and chipping off. It wouldn't surprise me if no one opened it since Leo left the maze years ago. I turned the doorknob and was happy to see that it wasn't locked, but the door was stuck shut. I put my weight against it and the door swung open.

The other side was completely different. It opened up into something that looked like the ruins of an old underground train station. It was dusty and dirty from God knows how many years of being buried and abandoned. The air felt stale as it hit my gills. As I scanned the area with my electric torch, scores of large rats scurried away into holes in the tile walls. Directly in front of me, there was a concrete trench with a set of train tracks stretching from one tunnel to the next. I climbed down and back up to the other side. There were abandoned shops and vending machines there. I picked up an old newspaper. It had an article about Supreme King Lucien Vidal when he was a mere senator. Oh, how times have changed! Reading that article from before my time probably bought me my ticket to be launched into space simply because it didn't paint him as an infallible person. I folded up the contraband and put it in my backpack. It's hidden under the floorboard behind the toilet in my apartment if you are interested in reading it yourself.

There was a staircase leading up and Leo's map indicated that my trek would continue at the top. When I finished climbing, the maze opened up into a sprawling underground city. I pointed my torch straight up and saw the dome covering me. It was a lost city literally covered up by our government and left in plain sight with nothing but fear and rumors to keep it hidden. I looked at my map again. The temple was a mere ten city blocks away. I pulled a red ribbon out of my pack and tied it to a nearby street lamp. I did this so I could easily find the stairs on my way back.

I walked the streets of that deserted city which were cracked and unkempt. It reminded me of Dubhaven. It had many of the same architectural styles and themes. Thinking back, I wonder if they are both relics of the same bygone era. Dubhaven built on top of itself while maintaining its ancient foundation while this city was covered up and faded from our memories.

The walk itself was uneventful save for a brief moment when I saw a towering black figure moving in the distance. I moved cautiously figuring that it was some kind of security robot. After a few more intersections, I headed east for another two blocks and there it was. The Temple in the Labyrinth stood before me. It had two flights of stairs that led to a huge set of doors. The building itself looked very sturdy and tall. The roof was intricate and had statues of little children with the wings of birds growing out of their backs. The top of the building angled up to a point and there was a letter "t" on top of that. I remember wondering if there were any other temples dedicated to other letters of the alphabet there.

The doors themselves were locked, but there was a colorful window that was broken, so I carefully climbed in that way. There was a small nondescript room in the front and beyond that was another set of large double doors. These were unlocked so I was able to walk right in. The back room was infinitely more interesting. There were rows upon rows of wooden benches. The back of each bench had the same two books in a little compartment. One was a book of odd, but uplifting songs. The other was a long novel of sorts. I haven't had the chance to read them, but I left a copy of each in my apartment if you are interested.

Beyond the benches there was a raised stage with an ornate podium on the side. On the other side of the stage there was an organ. I theorized that someone would play the organ and the people in the benches would sing the songs in the songbook. On the large wall behind the stage there was another enormous letter "t" mounted there. This one had a morbid copper statue of a skinny bearded man nailed to it. Upon further inspection, I noted that they had a thorned vine wrapped around their head and even though the statue was painstakingly detailed, the figure had no gills.

I figured that I would learn much more after reading the texts, so after I packed them into my bag, I left. The day was still young. I left the alphabet temple and continued down the dark road. Eventually, I came upon another large building. This one was far less ornate, but infinitely more interesting. This temple was dedicated to knowledge. It was a vast open room with hundreds of shelves. The shelves themselves were ten feet tall and filled with old books. I was amazed. Some of them were thousands of years old. I could have spent a millennia going from shelf to shelf learning about the past. There were even texts that dated back before Supreme King Lucien Vidal's time.

I devoured the information like a starved wolf would to a dead deer's carcass. In truth, fear of contraband and the threat of being launched into space had starved the minds of all of our people long ago. We have been conditioned by the elders to ignore our curiosity and accept the status quo. It is an obvious play for power and even I had been complicit with the practice for most of my life. There was no way I would pass my brain scan now. I learned so much and will have plenty of ideas to ponder as I float in the cold void. I hope this letter does the same for you, Rebecca.

Did you know we are not the first civilized species to live on this planet? There was a race of people who rose out of a different primordial soup than we did. They were honestly very much like us, but with one significant difference. They had a limited life span. They were not immortal like we are. They were called Homo sapiens, and they evolved from apes. Not the aquatic red apes that you and I are used to seeing, but the rare brown apes that still live deep in the jungle. The ones that die and reproduce frequently.

It's a fascinating idea. Two different primordial soups on the same planet existing millions of years apart producing species of plants and animals that coexist today. The ones that evolved from the first soup grew strong from a constant cycle of reproduction and death. This is why they breed like crazy and have short life spans. Each generation is a little bit better equipped to survive than the last. We come from the second soup. We don't die and we rarely reproduce. While I was reading those old texts in the dark, I learned about that second soup. The one that we evolved from. It actually came to be while that ancient civilization flourished.

There was a rebellious Homo sapien named John Peterson that became the genesis for our race. He belonged to a group called The Hot Skulls Gang. They were a biker gang. From what I can gather, biker gangs were nomadic tribes that rode around on motorized bicycles. During his travels, he ran into a gypsy Homo sapien in a store called Target. A gypsy is like a wizard or something. They were also nomadic. Homo sapiens were very superstitious and this gypsy put a curse on John Peterson. The gypsy's curse was that someday, he would bleed to death.

That wasn't the only oddity about John Peterson. He was also part of a secret government experiment. I am not clear of the details because it was classified, but it had something to do with overexposure to microwaves, LSD, and a soda named Mountain Dew. The government experiment made him immortal. This odd little science cocktail is why you and I have been alive the last hundred or so years.

Science is the meat in the soup, but the gypsy's curse is the broth. Here is how it happened:

John Peterson was riding on his motorcycle with the rest of the Hot Skulls on an icy highway one night after being experimented on and cursed. A tractor-trailer started skidding on the ice in front of them, and when it crashed, John Peterson couldn't stop his bike in time. He hit the truck at full force. The impact tore off his right arm and the blow he took to his head sent him into a coma.

The government experiment that made John Peterson immortal prevented him from dying, but the gypsy's curse was doing it's damndest to make him bleed to death. His blood would not clot. The result was a stalemate between magic and science. John Peterson simply bled. Forever.

The Hot Skulls tried to use a leather belt as a tourniquet on John's arm to stop the blood from flowing, but they didn't have any luck. The EMTs eventually arrived on the scene and whisked him away in their ambulance. They couldn't stop the bleeding either. By the time they made it to the hospital, the EMTs were ankle-deep in his blood. When the back doors of the ambulance opened, blood splashed onto the concrete ground like a waterfall.

The doctors in the ER never saw anything like it. They worked all night, but eventually had to evacuate the first floor of the hospital. Blood had seeped out under the doors in the operating room and it was no longer safe to be admitting new patients. Eventually it was decided by hospital administrators to attach a series of plastic dryer tubes that had been duct-taped together to John's wound. The other side of the makeshift plastic pipe was routed to a pond next to the hospital. By the time the pond was full to the brim with blood, the government had stepped in.

The government airlifted John's body to an isolated lab in the Mojave Desert. The entire trip, blood was being drained from the bottom of the jet onto the earth below. The scientists worked night and day to figure out a solution to this problem, while they drained the sanguine liquid out into the open desert. They hoped the blood would evaporate, but this was gypsy magic. The blood would not dry or clot.

***

During this time, there was a very powerful Homo sapien called the president. He ruled a large nation from a building called the White House. The war room in the White House was full of scientists, generals, and medical experts. It had been a month since John's unconscious body arrived in the government lab. The media found out what was going on three days earlier thanks to the Washington Times investigative reporting. It had become a big story. Here is what was said.

"Can't we just nuke the body?" Asked the president.

"That's a little extreme, don't you think?" Said one of the generals. "We can't just nuke away all our problems."

"I mean, it would solve the problem though, right? The body can't bleed if we incinerate it," said the president.

"That's the problem," said a scientist. "There's something strange going on with his cells. They are extremely resilient. I've exposed them to high levels of radiation and they don't deteriorate. I don't even see the cells living natural life cycles. They don't seem to die. You would think something like that would cause cancerous growths, but the body is only producing cells as they are needed. It needs to produce blood cells to clot the wound, but it isn't clotting, so it just keeps going and we can't dispose of the blood, because we can't kill the cells."

"I don't see the big deal," said the White House chief of staff. "Who cares if this dude keeps bleeding?"

"Current models show that in 611,532,467,532 years it could produce enough blood to fill the Grand Canyon," said another scientist.

"Just for context," said another scientist. "The sun will explode in 7,500,000,000 years."

"When's the next election?" Asked the president.

"Three years," said another senior staff member.

"Yeah, let's just throw it in the Grand Canyon," said the president.

"Sounds good to me," said the chief of staff.

So, they did. The government threw the body in the Grand Canyon and shut it down to the public. When that president left office, the new president wanted to launch Peterson's body into space, but congress deemed it too expensive, and it didn't get funding. The next two administrations didn't even address the issue.

****

A big war erupted after that. The Homo sapien world leaders decided to use atomic bombs against each other. Homo sapians were almost wiped from the Earth. They survived in a radioactive wasteland for a time by living in small tribes, but eventually, they died off. All the while, John Peterson's body slowly filled the Grand Canyon with blood.

****

This new primordial soup grew larger and larger for thousands of years. There were no more Homo sapiens to disturb the bleeding body. The cells began to evolve. First into blood fish, then amphibians, to reptiles, to mammals, to us, and all the immortal animals in between. All of our civilization can be traced back to the bleeding comatose body of John Peterson. That's the truth. We now know this fact, and it is the contraband that will have us exiled to space.

I made my way out of the building and began my trek out of the labyrinth. As I turned the corner on my way back to the abandoned train station, I saw that black figure again. This time it saw me too. It was a security bot, and a nasty one at that. Its designer had no shortage of macabre imagination because its appearance was frightening, and I still get goosebumps thinking about it. It was a 15-foot tall spider robot adorned with bull bones. In the place where the head should be, it had a bovine skull bolted to its front. I would be lying if I said I had a good look at it as it charged toward me in the darkness, but I saw that much.

I didn't know I could run as fast as I did, but the machine was still quicker than me. I could hear the grinding gears of it's joints and the hard impact of metal claws on concrete getting louder and louder. I kept my electric torch aimed forward frantically searching for the red ribbon I had tied to the street lamp in front of the train station. I am glad I found it because if I had hesitated at all, the machine would have caught up with me. I ran down the stairs almost in a controlled fall, trying to create distance. I reached the brown door and pulled with all my might to get it open. When I was back in the maze, I knew I was safe because there was no way that robot could fit through those narrow halls. I had done it. I braved the labyrinth and escaped unscathed. That is, until I get my next brain scan.

Rebecca, now you know the truth of our people's origin. I am not sure why the elders keep these secrets from us, but I am sure it is part of a larger plan to control us. I will finish this lengthy heretic letter and send it to you this afternoon. By the time you read it, I will be floating through space, observing the stars, and pondering my choices. I will also be thinking of you.

    With love and affection,
    -Archie Hall

BOOKS BY THIS AUTHOR

The Island Of Naked Women